HOPE

Project Animal Rescue

HOPE
Project Animal Rescue

By Alyssa Milano
with Debbie Rigaud
ILLUSTRATED BY ERIC S. KEYES

Scholastic Inc.

Library of Congress Cataloging-in-Publication Data available

ISBN 978-1-338-32941-4

10 9 8 7 6 5 4 3 2 1   20 21 22 23 24

Printed in the U.S.A.   23

First printing 2020
Book design by Katie Fitch

To Milo, Bella, and Luke! I love you. (A lot.)
—A.M.

For kids who answer the call
to rescue a friend in need.
—D.R.

To Autumn, Ian, Makayla, Kaitlyn, and Gracie.
—E.K.

HOPE

Project Animal Rescue

Chapter 1

My hand is an inch from grabbing the end of the leash, but it's dragged away when the scrappy Maltese pooch takes off running.

"Hey!" I shout at the playful dog. "Come back here!"

Who knew doggy daycare duty would be this busy? For once, the crashing ocean waves and seagull calls aren't the loudest sounds at this seaside dog park: It's the gleeful barking.

I take a step but stop short when a Doberman unexpectedly zips across my path. Her excitement makes me grin. I look both ways to make sure my path is clear. But when I take another step, that same Doberman comes up racing from behind, grazing my leg.

Then, before I can stop her, the Doberman picks up the end of the Maltese's leash.

"Let go of that!"

"Hope, check this out!" My sister, Marie, is walking toward me, smiling and holding a greasy brown paper bag. "This job has its perks. A customer brought us back fries to share."

I see it all happen in slow motion.

The moment Marie holds out the bag toward me,

the Doberman and the Maltese run toward her with the leash still stretched out between them. Marie trips right over it. I catch my tumbling sister, but the fries rain down all around us.

The handful of dogs nearest to us come racing over to feast.

We hold them back while picking up as many fries as we can. But even quicker than the dogs is one super aggressive seagull, its wings whipping way too close to our faces.

Of course, now more dogs come to chase away the seagull, which we 100 percent welcome.

It's a hilarious disaster.

My best friend, Sam, runs over from her section and manages to help us clean up the chaos before things get as out of control as our laughter.

So many paws, so little pause.

We've been at this beachside dog park for one hour, and the bowwow brigade just keeps coming. Blame it on this sunny Sunday. It turned out to be the perfect weather for my doggy daycare fund-raiser.

"We're so glad you're trusting your best friend to us," I tell yet another customer who is checking in yet another dog. This time it's a man in bright green shorts and colorful sunglasses to match. He hands me the equally bright yellow leash, which his Jack Russell terrier immediately tugs. Good thing I'm holding tight. *This isn't my first rodeo, pup. I was trained by my own dogs.* "Enjoy your lunch, and we'll make sure little Frankie here gets the exercise she needs."

"Thank you," says the man as he crouches and gives Frankie one last nuzzle.

"No, thank *you* for your donation to the Eastern Shore Animal Shelter," I reply, sticking to the script I memorized and repeat to everyone. "All the doggy daycare proceeds go toward helping the shelter stay open."

"Oh no." The man stands with a frown. "I didn't realize they were closing. Do you know when?"

"They're supposed to close in about two months."

"Well, here's hoping there's more than enough time for you to save the shelter," he says.

"The support we're getting today from people like you gets us closer," my chipper outer voice answers. My inner voice is way less confident. *What if I can't squeeze in enough doggy daycare hours to make a difference?* It's a good thing Sam, Marie, and my parents have agreed to help in any way they can. Maybe I can get them to cover two other dog parks when I'm back here next weekend.

"Well, thanks for watching Frankie. She's a sucker for the ocean, but we spoke about the waves being too rough today for a swim, didn't we, Frankie?" The man slides his shades down his nose to give a warning glare to his excited pup. Frankie looks away, checking out the playful scene around her. Her dad leans toward me and whispers, "She'll make a run for the water if you don't stay close."

I nod like a soldier. "We got this."

I wave goodbye and smile politely, even though my mind is racing. It's already been a few weeks since Marie announced that the shelter where our family adopted our tiny terrier, Cosmo, and giant mutt, Rocket, is closing. The news hit me hard. Thinking about what would happen to the hungry, homeless, or abused pets in the area without this shelter made my heart hurt. I can't imagine the feeling of waiting to be rescued. It makes me want to rush out and save them all myself.

As bummed as I was to hear about the shelter, I couldn't do anything about it then. My science club crew had entered the annual science competition, and I had to work around the clock to help get our project done. That meant helping build a miniature amusement park, programming a homemade robot, and settling some differences we girls had with most of the boys in the science club.

Everything went horribly wrong with the project we'd worked on. Thankfully, we managed to make our goof—okay, it was mostly *my* goof— part of the presentation. The judges appreciated our message that mistakes play a huge role in scientific discoveries, and our teacher, Mr. Gillespie, was impressed we'd made lemonade from some seriously sour lemons.

My science club buddies Camila, Grace, Henry, and I got to go up on the competition stage with the rest of our members to accept our honorable mention ribbons. Mr. Gillespie even brought me up to speak on everyone's behalf. It's hard to believe all that was just a little over a week ago.

Not long after that, I contacted the shelter and volunteered to do this doggy daycare fund-raiser for the next few Sundays. I explained that it had all been cleared by a parks department official. (Luckily, that official is a fan of my mom's downtown art gallery!) The woman I emailed at the shelter seemed resigned to the shutdown yet still touched to have the support. "Every little bit counts," she had said.

You just never know.

That's what I keep telling myself. You never know if something you do will snowball into something bigger and greater. I'm hoping this daycare fund-raiser raises not only money, but also awareness. The way I picture it—or, more accurately, daydream it—if I talk up the shelter to enough people, people will unite, take action, and demand the shelter stay open.

"Do we have another *paw-some* customer?" Sam calls out from across the dog park. She already looks exhausted from wrangling pups in this heat. There's a dusty paw print stamped on her pink T-shirt. She's been working so hard. I'm grateful she's been able to lend a hand, even though she needs to leave early to rehearse for our school's fall musical.

"Yup. Sam, meet Frankie," I say as Frankie runs circles around me, tying me up in her own leash. I manage to unravel myself just as a longhaired golden retriever charges for me.

"Down, buddy," I scold the eager retriever.

Is he after the special homemade treats Camila made? I'm carrying the baggie of dog-shaped biscuits in my front pocket. I make a mental note to tell Camila her new recipe is a hit with the pups.

But no. He's going for the stick in my *back* pocket. I forgot all about our game of fetch when Frankie's owner arrived. I grab the stick and toss it as far as possible. The retriever darts after it. Next, I unleash Frankie and watch her chase after the retriever.

"This place is busier than the space center on rocket launch day!" says Sam. "Any chance there's a last-minute space mission happening that your dad forgot to mention to you?"

"No, he wouldn't forget to tell me something that important." My dad knows how much I love all things science. He's a rocket scientist who works for NASA. It never gets old saying that, just like it never gets old for residents of our Cape Canaveral, Florida, hometown to gather for a rocket launch viewing. I shrug. "Everyone's just excited it hasn't rained in hours, is all."

"True," says Sam, smiling at the way Frankie is suddenly rolling around in the cool grass. The retriever comes barreling back, and Sam takes a step out of the way.

I suck in ocean air, then shriek. "Watch where you step!"

"Ew!" Sam squeals when she realizes how close her foot has come to the pile of dog poop in her path. It's a good thing Sam is so graceful. She skips over the pile like the trained dancer she is.

I shake my head. "That was way too close!"

"I thought I'd picked up after all the dogs I'm watching . . ." Sam searches the pack in one neck-twisting motion. "Hey, where's your sister?"

I roll my eyes. "Follow the crowd. Marie is way more about the humans than the dogs lately." As in, ever since she started high school. My sister was always popular, but now when she hangs out with me, it's like it's a chore for her. Like today. I'm starting to think she's only here because she promised Mom and Dad she'd help.

We spot Marie leaning against a fence, chatting to a group of high school kids on the other side of it. She jogs away from them to greet a returning customer coming to pick up their dog. The group of teenagers moves on.

"How is it that she's friends with every other person walking by this dog park?" Sam asks in wide-eyed awe.

I give the retriever a homemade doggy snack for waiting patiently this time instead of jumping on me. Of course, that grabs the attention of other greedy goobers who want a snack, too. I giggle at the sight of them trotting over with their tongues hanging.

"Can you imagine what JFK Middle would be like today if Marie hadn't graduated last year?" I wonder, handing out one snack per dog and sending them back to play. Sam and I just started sixth grade there.

"You tell me." Sam smirks at me.

I don't even have to think about it. "It would be unbearable. Middle school is hard enough without having to deal with your big sister's fan club. Did I mention teachers still stop me in the hall to ask me how she's doing?"

"Look at it this way—we know someone Cape Canaveral famous! She's like our very own influencer, in the flesh."

"Humph," I scoff, grabbing up the pooper scooper I brought from home and picking up what Marie should have. Two pups are in a tug-of-war over a squeaky toy, and Sam separates them. "Admit it," she says, holding the toy over her head. "You've benefited from her influencer status."

"That denim skirt I wore on the first day of school did look super cute," I say through a sneaky smile. "Fine, I admit it. But knowing Marie, she's not

talking about the shelter. She's going on and on about music or some sale at the mall."

"Hey, Marie!" another friend calls to my sister.

At least Marie is great at multitasking. She's chatting with a friend while reuniting a dog with its human parent.

"The beach volleyball game is one person short," the friend is saying to Marie. "You should get in on this epic matchup."

As Marie chats, Frankie, who'd been lingering by the front gate, slips out and bolts toward the ocean.

"Frankie!" I shriek and run toward the gate, pausing for a moment to make sure Sam has me covered.

"Go, go, go! I'll watch the dogs," Sam shouts.

Marie doesn't hesitate. She's hot on Frankie's tail, kicking up beach sand with each step. Watching her reminds me of the time she came running when I cried after a playground bully pushed me to the ground and called me a *Hope*-less nerd. Marie's always had my back, just like she does now.

And thank goodness she's a way faster runner than me. Also, yes, it turns out that I'm lucky she's got tons of friends at the beach. She double-teams with one of the boys she was talking to earlier. Together, they corner Frankie until I arrive and scoop her up in my arms.

"Whew!" Everyone at the beach cheers and pets Frankie.

The walk back to the dog park with Marie is way less festive.

I can feel Marie wearing her guilt like a heavy backpack. She's pressing her fingers against one side of her stomach, like she's got a stitch in her side from running so hard. "Hope, I'm so sorry," she says sincerely. "I totally didn't see the little guy was behind me."

"More like you didn't pay attention," I grumble.

"And Frankie is a girl."

"I didn't mean for this to happen. It was an accident."

Sam beams when she sees us. "Awesome job! That was quick."

"Thank you, *Sam*." Marie rolls her eyes at me and heads back to her post.

I turn to Sam. "Next time," I puff, "remind me to ask Marie to wear a disguise so people don't recognize her."

She cracks up, but I hold a finger to my mouth and shush her.

"Too soon," I whisper, which only makes Sam laugh again. Frankie seems to chuckle right along with her, which makes me grin. Sam grabs her mini backpack and gives me a goodbye hug.

"My mom is waiting for me by the pier," Sam says. And then, half serious, she asks, "Can I trust you not to be at each other's throats while I'm gone?"

"We're good. Thank you so much for helping," I say. "Now, go—break a leg."

"It's rehearsals, not opening night," Sam chuckles.

Thankfully, after Sam leaves, the doggy drop-offs

slow down and the park gets calmer. By the time Marie's friend Diya and Diya's mom pick us up, we've made about $200 in payments and donations. I count it in the car on the ride home.

I can hear Marie and Diya chatting in the third row behind me. "How many doggy daycare Sundays will you be doing?" Diya asks my sister. "Maybe I can get a few friends to bring down their pups."

"Uh, not now," whispers Marie.

"Why all the secrecy?" I turn around and ask.

"I was going to tell you later," Marie answers awkwardly. "Earlier at the park, I ran into a friend who volunteers at the shelter, and she said they moved up their last day. They're closing on the twenty-fifth now."

"The twenty-fifth of what month?"

"This month," Marie says softly, already looking sorry to be the one to break the news to me . . . again.

Did I hear that right?

"But today's the thirteenth!" I shout.

My words ricochet off a wall of awkward silence, and then disappear into the steady hum of the car's motor.

What chance do those shelter dogs have now?

Chapter 2

Less than two weeks until the shelter closes? The thought forms a lump in my throat.

What will happen to all the poor pups who live there?

As soon as I unlock the front door of our home, Diya's mom drives off. I'm kind of relieved Marie and Diya decided to hang out at the coffee shop in town with the rest of the cool kids. I'm all for things being quieter at home right now. My sister doesn't know how loud she can be—especially when she's plugged into her dance music. There's no telling how earsplitting her off-key howling would be this time, and I can't afford distractions while I'm thinking up an emergency fund-raising strategy.

With tongues hanging and tails wagging, Cosmo and Rocket greet me at the door. Today, I keep my hug going for way longer than usual. Rocket starts trying to squirm her ginormous body free, while Cosmo settles into the crook of my arm and closes his eyes.

Just thinking about these two fluff butts being in the same predicament as the one the Eastern Shore's dogs are in right now makes me want to stay close to them.

My parents must've heard the front door slam. "Marie? Hope?" Mom calls out, her voice wafting into the house from outside.

"Hi! It's just me!" I shout, rising to my feet with Cosmo in my arms.

"We're out back, sweetie! Join us?"

"In a minute," I singsong my reply. "I need to do something first."

From my arms, Cosmo looks down his nose at Rocket. The big, lovable mutt stares back, staying put as we head down the long hallway. I breeze by a blur of hung artwork and our fave family photo, where Dad is smiling with spinach in his teeth. Then I zip past the KEEP OUT! sign on Marie's door. Across the hall is my room—or, as I like to call it in times like these, my lab.

Every future scientist needs to document her findings. Filming video diaries is my way of doing this. I make a beeline to my desk and grab my new cell phone tripod from the top drawer. When Rocket hears the rattling of the box of treats I keep in there, she trots into the room expecting to be fed. Cosmo jumps out of my arms and begs for a treat, too.

"How can I say no to those faces?" I sigh, tossing them each a crunchy bone-shaped bite.

As soon as I adjust the phone on its little stand, I check my look, then slide my headband away from my forehead. I back away from the camera until my out-to-there hair is in the frame. "Good enough,"

I say, flashing a nose-crinkling smile. There's a glint in my eyes, thanks to the sunrays beaming through my window.

I set the camera timer, and when it gets to zero, I start talking.

"Day one of doggy daycare," I announce to the camera. "The good news: It was a success. We raised close to two hundred dollars for the shelter." My smile fades and I take a deep breath. "The oh-no-say-it-ain't-so news: The shelter is closing in *twelve days*. Two weeks is enough time to cram for an exam or plan a surprise party. But to fund-raise?"

I shake my head and start pacing. In case a treat falls out my pocket, Cosmo and Rocket keep in step with my pacing, back and forth, then back and forth all over again.

"We need to raise thousands of dollars, and with a shorter deadline, doggy-sitting our way there just won't cut it. For one, it's way too exhausting." I stop short, and Cosmo and Rocket slam into the backs of my legs. "I need to do more. But what could I possibly do to make a difference in such a short time?"

Where do I even start?

At the science competition, I failed miserably when I tried to be a solo-flying hero. Nope. Being on a one-girl mission to save the shelter won't work. Just as suddenly as my pacing halted, my roving eyes stop and zero in on the collection of Galaxy Girl comic books sitting on my bookshelf.

"What would Galaxy Girl do?"

That's it! I've got to make like Galaxy Girl in issue 24!

"She'd assemble a team of do-gooders like she did when the evil Mechantra's interstellar army was too mighty to defeat on her own," I announce to Cosmo and Rocket, who don't look thrilled with how empty my wildly waving hands are right now. "And I'm talking a team of more than just Mom, Dad, Marie, and Sam."

I catch sight of a notepad tucked between the

stack of comic books and a science trophy. I walk over to grab it.

"This calls for more organized, detailed planning—not to mention, deep analysis," I say once I'm back in front of the camera with the notepad and pen. I plop down on my bed and open to a clean page.

"A checklist never hurts," I say, ready to dictate what I'm thinking. The first thing that pops into my mind is "rescue the rescues."

My pen is on the move. *"Mission: Rescue the Rescues."* On the bottom of the page, I leave room for a *List of People to Ask for Help* and *Ideas for Fund-raisers.* "Okay, first thing I can do right this minute is *Update Mom and Dad.*"

I'm grateful my parents and my sister have agreed to be a part of my fund-raising. I just hope they can now do more—and in a lot less time. I get up and walk over to the camera. "Signing off for now. Wish me luck!"

With Rocket and Cosmo at my heels, and my checklist in hand, I head to the backyard and find my parents lounging by the pool in a rare moment of chillaxation. Once we step foot—and paw—outside, Cosmo goes off chasing a bird, and Rocket finds a shaded area to rest in.

I hate to interrupt their reading (Mom) and napping (Dad), but I have to update them on the doggy daycare haul, the moved-up deadline, and the need for *urgent* help.

"We only have about two weeks." I poke at the air with my pen. "I know we spoke about how everyone can pitch in, but I'll be calling on you sooner than I thought."

"Hope, there's no need to worry about us," says Dad, now wide-awake and all in. "We've signed on, and we're not turning back or changing our minds."

"Thank you," I say, relieved.

Check.

"What about Marie?" Mom asks.

"She's signed on . . . or she will be," I say, wincing. I realize I haven't spelled out to Marie what the tighter deadline means for our efforts. Marie doesn't do hints. You have to be as clear as possible with her, because she won't fill in the blanks for you. The girl just won't meet you halfway, even if she knows what you're hinting at.

"Well, she helped today—in her own way. And I assume she'll keep that up."

I guess. I hope.

"Good."

Check.

"And my next step is to see what else Sam can do—and to get our friends on board, too."

"Before giving your friends their marching orders," Mom says, in that way that makes me lean in, because judging from her tone, I know she's about to say something key, "you should visit the shelter first to find out exactly what *they* need."

"Yeah, for sure," I say. "That's a good place to start." And I'll be ready to do just that first thing after school tomorrow.

I've been in the hot sun enough for one day, but I love hanging by the pool. I grab my phone out of my back pocket and slide into the Adirondack chair positioned in the shade of a palm tree.

Hi guys! I text my friends, continuing the thread

we'd started when Sam invited everyone to her house to binge-watch the second season of our new favorite TV show.

Hey! the girls answer one after another.

Great day at the dog park today. We raised $200! I add a celebration streamers emoji for good measure.

Of course, Lacy is the first to respond with positivity. She never misses a chance to boost a friend.

Amazing! Lacy texts with a string of high five emojis.

I send a sad face emoji. *Too bad it's not amazing enough. I found out the shelter closes in 12 days,* I text back.

NOOOO! responds Golda. Golda is usually chill in our accelerated classes, but sometimes I wonder why she hasn't joined Sam and Lacy in the school musical. She can be just as theatrical as they can.

That's horrible! Camila responds next.

I'm so sorry, Hope, texts Grace.

More details to come, but can I lean on you guys to help?

Definitely! writes Charlie.

We got you! Sam finally chimes in.

Sam, can you come with me to the shelter tomorrow to drop off our donations? I text back.

I think so. Meet me in the auditorium after school!

Thanks! ☺

New item on the checklist: team up, act fast, and save the shelter.

Chapter 3

"**A**ren't you forgetting something?" my dad yells out the car window after I've slammed the rear door shut.

Am I?

We've just pulled up to JFK Middle School. It's

on the early side, but a few kids are already milling around on the front lawn. I have to hurry if I'm going to catch Camila before first period. But just in case Dad's right, I unzip my backpack and rummage through everything inside in a calm panic.

Don't tell me I forgot my checklist!

I chill as soon as I spot the purple-and-pink notebook.

"Whew!" I pull it out and hug it to my chest.

"No, I think I've got everything," I say as I thread my arms back through my backpack's straps and turn toward school.

"That's not what you forgot." Dad's using his mopey tone—and face—now.

"Dad, you're dragging this out," Marie huffs from the front passenger seat. I guess that means Marie is *not* asleep. With her shades being so tinted and her body so slumped the entire car ride over, it's been tough to tell.

"Oh!" I pivot on my rubber soles and face the car. "Bye, Dad! Have a great day! See you later!" I wave my hand in the air, and Dad finally chuckles. "Sorry about that. Just eager to brainstorm with my friends.

We only have eleven days, so . . ."

Dad's smile says I'm forgiven. "I thought the plan was to find out what the shelter needs first."

"What it *needs* is for me to jump-start a plan right away, like, now!"

"Your friends are gonna just love hearing that first thing on a Monday morning." Marie faces me, one eyebrow raised high above her black sunnies. I can feel her scanning me up and down, with extra shade directed at the notepad in my hand.

"It's not like I'm going to lead with that," I say, my nose in the air and my eyes avoiding my sister's.

"They're going to see you coming a mile away," mumbles Marie. "Way to scare them off."

"She's passionate, is what she is," Dad says proudly.

"Sure, but no need to overdo it," Marie points out. "Learn to chill. Or better yet, be honest with yourself. There's really not enough time to pull this off."

"Bye, Marie!" I show her my back.

"Don't say I didn't warn you." Marie's voice floats out the car as Dad pulls away.

Her words rattle in my mind moments later

when I catch my friend Camila in the hall. She's just walked out of the girls' bathroom.

"Camila! Wait up." I jog up to her. She whips around, her long brown hair swatting at me in the process.

"Oh, hey." She looks relieved—in more ways than one. "I'm glad it's you. Because if another person shoves a cupcake in my face, I think I'll scream . . ."

"That sounds more like a dream than a nightmare." I smile.

"Yeah, well, you didn't just spend all weekend helping your dad fill an order of three hundred cupcakes for a picky customer's quinceañera."

I get Camila's frustration. She's told me and Grace some serious horror stories about the many bridezillas, groomzillas, and hostzillas she's had to deal with at her family's bakery.

"Every party starts off with the same harmless excitement you see here," she warns me, gesturing around the hallway. "But one wrong move and people will chew your head clean off."

To be fair, it is kinda crazy how overexcited everyone is about next Friday's Fall Formal. There are so many dance posters plastering the walls that the flyers for the school elections that went up last week are hardly noticeable. And everywhere you look, there seems to be a sign-up table, raffle station, or bake sale set up to support it. *Looks like I'm not the only eager one getting a jump start on fund-raising.*

I want to go to the formal, but I haven't been able to give it much thought. And now that the big dance is happening the same day the shelter is set to close, I'm not sure I'll have time. For a second, I imagine what it would be like if the Fall Formal posters were all about saving the shelter instead. *Aww, cute puppy dog faces everywhere.* I bite my lower lip to keep from jumping into my Rescue the Rescues pitch.

Learn to chill.

"That's a lot of drama for a birthday party," I say instead. Because it's true.

Camila notices the notebook I'm still clutching to my chest.

Your friends are going to see you coming a mile away.

"So, what else did you get up to this weekend?" I ask, because it feels like a tiny, invisible Marie is sitting on my shoulder, judging me.

I slowly lower that arm and loosen my grip on the notebook. We begin our stroll down a corridor crowded with Fall Formal sign-up tables. Camila takes a breath and prepares for the onslaught.

"Nothing, it was *all* cupcakes—kinda like this hallway," she says, eyeing the activity surrounding us. "Did the entire school decide to come in early today?" She points her chin at me. "Speaking of, what's your story?"

"I got ready early and caught a ride with my dad." *Learn to chill. Learn to chill. Learn to—* "Because I just couldn't sleep in when the shelter needs so much help!" I blurt out. "If we sit on this, it'll be too late."

"Want to sign up for the Fall Formal decorating committee?" A girl waves a clipboard in front of me. I thank her but shake my head no. The girl doesn't seem to notice how close Camila has come to blowing her lid.

"And I won't be fine knowing I didn't try my best to save those dogs," I continue without missing a beat. "So what do you say, Camila? Have some time now to brainstorm fund-raising ideas with me?"

"Cupcake?" asks a boy set up at the following table.

"Maybe another time." I smile politely at him as I listen for Camila's answer to my question.

"Hope, you know I got you, and I wish I could help right now," she says. "But I forgot to check on my larvae Friday. If I don't swing by the lab before science class, most of them won't make it. Okay if we talk later?"

I nod and Camila rushes off, her curtain of hair working hard to keep up with her.

When I get to my Advanced Science class a little later, I sit with my pen hovering over my ideas notebook. But after a few minutes I've got nothing. Maybe the problem is it's too empty and quiet in here.

There's usually so much thinking power in this room; you can practically hear the cogs grinding in everyone's brains.

Einstein seems to be taunting me from across the room. I usually like sitting in front of the playful poster of the famous scientist sticking out his tongue. But today, it seems like he's picking up where Marie left off. He has the same taunting look she had this morning when she told me I don't have enough time to pull this off.

"That's just Marie's theory, Einstein," I say, looking into his wild eyes.

I wish I felt as confident as I sound. The clock

face on the wall seems to be ticking double time. I know it's only my imagination, but my twisting tummy seems to think it's real.

I look back to the poster and imagine what Einstein might say.

It couldn't hurt to offer the shelter more fund-raising ideas.

"True, I didn't think of that," I say, relieved for the help.

When I go to the shelter after school to drop off the doggy daycare money and find out what else they need, maybe I can offer a few helpful ideas, too. After all, Galaxy Girl always comes prepared.

I finally touch pen to paper and, out of desperation, scribble the first fund-raising ideas that come to mind.

More doggy daycares.

Pet grooming party.

Dog walking services.

My fingers dig deep into my big hair and find my scalp. All the head massaging and pen drumming doesn't convince me that these ideas will get us very far in eleven days. All it does is spring coily strands right into my face.

I blow them back with a puff of breath. "I need brainstorm troopers."

Let's see.

"I know Camila has to go to the bakery after school, but maybe Grace can come to the shelter with me and Sam today," I say, pointing my drumstick slash pen at Einstein. "We can all think up better ideas on our walk over."

Perfect!

And suddenly, Einstein and I are not alone. Shep from science club walks in and does a curious eyeball scan around the room in search of my conversation

partner. I put my chat with Einstein on permanent pause.

"Ba-ba-di-da," I sing to myself, like that's what I'd been doing all along. *Not talking to a poster. Nope.* My drumstick pen is now a conductor's wand. I wave it a little before setting it down, putting away my notebook and pulling out my science textbook.

"Da-di-dum."

More people begin entering the room, including our teacher, Mr. Gillespie. Camila races in the moment the bell rings and takes her seat beside me. As Mr. Gillespie promptly begins lecturing, I make a thumbs-up as a wordless question to Camila. She nods yes, and I'm glad her larvae are still in the game.

My fund-raising mission may be in the larval stage right now, but I'm still in the game, too.

♡🐺☆

"Ms. Roberts, are we to assume you're pausing for dramatic effect?" Mr. Gillespie asks, looking right at me.

Did I miss something?

The class giggles. I can make out Connor snickering in the chuckle chorus. By now, I've got an ear for his rude remarks and snarky jokes. Making fun of me and calling out my mistakes in a super embarrassing and public way used to be his favorite pastime. That was before I finally stood up to him and put him in his place. Connor is still bitter that I brought up his famous scientist mom in front of the whole science club in that argument. (How could I have known she'd left his family for another genius?) But things *have* been better since we settled our differences after the science competition. He's not interrupting me and the other girls in class or in science club as much as he used to. Or maybe it's just his sidekick, Shep, who's been way cooler these days. Whatever. I have more pressing things to worry about.

"Earth to Hope," Camila whispers next to me.

"Oh, sorry," I say to Mr. Gillespie. "I was just working out an entirely different problem in my mind."

Thank goodness the question of the day is scrawled across the whiteboard. I look down to my opened textbook and quickly scan the last paragraph. The answer leaps to the tip of my tongue.

"Biodiversity."

"Very well done," praises Mr. Gillespie.

I lean back in my desk and let out a sigh of relief.

I catch Connor's eyes. His lips slide to the side of his face, where they

usually are when he's annoyed by my winning in class, in social situations, or in life in general.

Yup. Connor's attitude is the very least of my worries—if I could even classify it as a worry.

For the rest of class, I hang on to Mr. Gillespie's every word . . . just in case.

At the bell, Camila and I meet up with Grace down the hall and head to our next class together.

"Sorry I couldn't make your brainstorming sesh, Hope," says Camila.

"It's cool, your future painted lady butterflies needed you more," I say with a smile.

"How did the brainstorming go?" Grace asks over her shoulder. She's a little ahead of us because she's better at weaving through the JFK Middle crowds.

"It didn't," I call out to Grace. "But if you're free to come with me, I'm hoping we can have one on our walk to the shelter after school?" I wince as I wait for her answer.

"I can't today," says Grace. "I have an appointment."

"Oh yeah, your—oops." I miss a head-on collision with another girl by a hair, literally. "Your eye doctor appointment, right?"

I remember Grace talking about needing to get

new eyeglasses. The ones she's already wearing look supercool to me.

Grace's answer is muffled by loud whoops. We stop when we hit a human roadblock—two cheerleaders . . . cheering.

Camila rolls her eyes. "Ugh, you see what I mean? The Fall Formal raffle ticket winners are about to start a riot."

Grace says something surprising. "You guys want to enter the next drawing?"

"No, thank you," answers Camila, grimacing. "I'm not chancing it with that mob."

Grace's face falls, and the corridor now clear, she continues leading the way to class.

I wonder what's got her so bummed.

I'm sure my face looks a lot like Grace's right now. I'm bummed she can't come with me to the shelter, either.

But nope—I can't feel sorry for myself. Not when I need to make so much progress pitching in with the fund-raising.

Attempting to shake this off, I stick my tongue way out, just like Einstein. Making a silly face makes me feel a little better.

Camila and Grace catch me doing it and burst out laughing. I give them a fake offended pout at first, and then crack up with them.

Yup, I feel better. It'll all work out. I hope.

Chapter 4

The after-school bell is music to my ears. I almost start dancing when I hear it. The only thing left to do before I go to the shelter is meet up with Sam in the auditorium.

When I walk in, there's lots of activity onstage. Everyone seems so creative—the cast singing and acting onstage, the crew building and painting the backdrop. An adult in the first row jumps out of her seat and starts waving her arms like she's about to go airborne. And I don't even think she's the choreographer. From what I can tell, she's just instructing the cast where to stand onstage.

I take a seat a few rows back and watch. Moments later, I'm absorbed by the scene onstage. Sam is playing the demanding kid sister to the main character. She's so convincing as the bratty tattler that I crack up—out loud! I have to cover my mouth and hold my sides. The spotlights aren't even on, but my best friend is shining up there. My cheeks hurt

from smiling so hard with pride. Maybe that's why I don't even notice when Henry Chen, one of the seventh graders from science club, walks up to me.

"Hope?"

"Oh, hey, Henry!" I try not to sound so happy to see his cute—er, friendly—face. "Are you in the musical?"

"No, I'm part of the crew."

Henry was amazing at building the mini amusement park for our science club presentation, so I'm not surprised he's helping design the drama club's set, too. I couldn't tell from his outfit, though. Most stage crew members are wearing black shirts and black leggings or jeans. Henry's got on one of his everyday basketball jerseys and shorts. But to his credit, he *is* wearing a black jersey.

"Are *you* in the musical?" he asks without a hint of doubt in his voice, and I appreciate that. When people see Sam and me, they easily classify me as the awkward one. Sam's the outgoing one with all the friends. But that's been slowly changing ever since I started JFK Middle and met Camila and Grace.

I smile. "I'm here to drag my best friend, Sam, with me to the animal shelter. It's in danger of shutting down, so we're going to go over there and figure out a plan of action."

"Cool, I'm glad you're doing something. If you need more volunteers, let me know," he offers.

"That's so nice of you, thanks!" I say, before Henry walks back to the rest of the set crew.

Lacy spots me from the wings of the stage. She waves and bounds over to meet me.

"Hey!" Lacy holds her hands in the air, inviting me to double high-five her. I slap her palms and smile at her sweet enthusiasm. She's so genuinely welcoming and cool. I might not have found that out if it weren't for us reconnecting through Sam.

"You're super supportive, coming to see Sam rock the stage," Lacy tells me.

"Aw, no."

"Yes, you are, and I love it."

I don't have the heart to tell her I meant no, as in *"No, that's not why I'm here."* But Lacy's right—it is cool to see Sam in her element. I know the feeling of having friends show up to see you at your best. And it is awesome to see how things with the musical are coming together now, even if that's not why I came.

"Oops . . . Sam's scene is over," Lacy says, peering like a meerkat. "That means my part's coming up. Catch you later!"

"See ya!"

As Lacy climbs up the stage steps, an extra happy Sam jumps off them and practically skips over. "Hope!"

She throws her arms around me, and I hug her back just as tight.

"You looked amazing up there!" I squeal, and then she squeals. When we pull away, I notice Sam doesn't have her backpack, and she doesn't look ready to go.

Sam grimaces. "I'm sorry, but the director asked

me to stay longer, so I can't come with you to the animal shelter."

Before I can control it, I pout and make a whiny sound.

Guess I'm on my own today.

"But I promise to go with you next time," Sam says.

I stick my tongue out, Einstein style, and then nod. "Okay, I'll take you up on that."

Or maybe I won't. It'll save me from disappointment. With everyone so caught up in their own worlds, it looks like getting actual helping hands will be tougher than I thought.

♡🐺☆

Eastern Shore Animal Shelter is a short walk from school. It sits far back from the main road, behind a tall bush that's been allowed to grow wild. If you're not careful, you can walk right past it. As I enter the parking area, I can hear some of the dogs running around in the large backyard.

It's been over two years since I was here last, when we took Rocket and Cosmo home for the first time. As soon as I step inside, I notice how much has changed since then. For one, it seems brighter . . . cleaner. There's a neat, updated front desk in the main entrance now, instead of the old, cluttered one. The young woman standing behind it greets me with the widest smile I've ever seen on any face. She's in a turquoise T-shirt with the shelter's logo on it. I read the name tag pinned to it and introduce myself.

"Hi, Ms. Keely Aquino? I'm Hope Roberts—the one who's been emailing you about fund-raising," I say, holding out my hand in greeting. My parents

would probably telepathically get some emergency signal if I didn't speak clearly, make eye contact, and offer a polite greeting to Ms. Keely. They are always going on about stuff like that.

The dachshund-shaped charms on the woman's earrings swing as she nods while pumping my hand. "Yes, Hope—wonderful to meet you in person," she says with a wider-than-wide smile.

Ms. Keely is the kind of person who is cool and warm at the same time. I instantly like her. "Thanks for making time to meet with me."

"Of course!" she says with a gasp in her voice. "I was so impressed with your email, and with the way you turned your concerns into real action. I'd love to give you a little tour of the shelter. Consider it my small way of saying thank you."

My face must look all gushing emoji right now. It

feels so good to know what I did was helpful to Ms. Keely and the shelter, at least on some level.

She rests her elbows on the front desk and leans in my direction. "But first, tell me, how are your sweet rescue dogs doing?" she asks.

"That's so cool of you to remember them," I say, beaming with my whole self.

"Oh, even from your email, I could tell you wanted to go on and on about them."

"But I didn't want to get carpal tunnel." We both chuckle.

"Well, they sound like amazing dogs. I can see why this shelter is so special to you."

I nod. "When I heard you might close, I wanted to do all I could to help."

"We are truly grateful for your support," she says, her smile going right back to covering half her face. I catch a hint of sadness in her eyes before she blinks it away.

"Oh! Before I forget." I hand her the envelope I've just taken from my bag. "Here's hoping this will get you closer to your goal."

Ms. Keely looks touched as she accepts the envelope full of donations. Her bronze face beams so bright, the freckles on her cheeks nearly glint like stars. "Thank you. Every little bit counts, Hope."

It could just be me, but the way she says "little" feels extra tiny. That must mean they're really in

deep. *I gotta ask . . .*

"Ms. Keely, how much does the shelter need to stay open?"

Her shoulders slump way down, and her big smile slides off her face. "We need twenty thousand dollars," she says.

Chapter 5

I replay Ms. Keely's words in my head. Did I hear that amount right? The shelter needs *how much* to stay open?

"As in *twenty thousand dollars*?" I ask.

Ms. Keely gives me a sympathetic smile. She comes around the counter and leans against it, her arms crossed.

"I know. It's a lot to process."

Both my eyebrows jump. "Yeah, it is."

"The truth is, it takes a lot of money to keep this place running, plus to take care of the animals. And sadly, we just lost one of our biggest sponsors, whom we relied on for the bulk of our support."

When Ms. Keely shakes her head, her messy updo threatens to come undone.

"Boy." I feel gut-punched. My backpack suddenly feels heavier than it did a second ago. I slide it down my arms and lay it at my feet.

"Hey, I recognize that look," Ms. Keely says. "I don't let myself dwell on the magnitude of it all." Her fingers poke at the air, like she's chipping away at something. "'A vast universe of troubles can be taken on one foe at a time.'"

If I were a dog, my ears would so flicker right now. I'd recognize that Galaxy Girl quote anywhere! "Are you a Galaxite, too?" I press down on my chest with both hands, as if to keep from jumping with excitement.

Her eyes go big and round. "Since the very first issue! You?"

"So much yes!" I grin almost as wide as she does.

"I should've known. Galaxites are unstoppable when they set their hearts on something. My focus now is on the big adoption event we're holding at the beach on Wednesday afternoon."

Now her finger points toward the poster taped to the wall behind the visitor sign-in sheet. I pull out my phone and take a picture of it.

"We could use a few more volunteers," says Ms. Keely. "Know anyone who'd be interested?"

"I am, and I can ask a few of my friends!" I quickly text the poster pic to my friend group chat with the question: *Who's in?*

"Perfect! Meet me there at four?"

I nod like a preschooler who has been offered candy. Ms. Keely gives me a high five.

"Awesome. Now let's start that tour I promised you," she says. "Can I leave your backpack here for you?"

"Thanks!" I hold on to my phone and hand my bag to her. She stuffs it into one of the lobby desk's cubbyholes.

She pops into the front office to let someone in there know she'll be stepping away. Not many visitors are coming in and out right now. But that could just be because of the time of day.

She points herself toward to the door, like she's a soccer player and the door's the goal. Her messy updo almost comes undone. "Right this way."

I follow behind her like—well, a puppy dog. She leads me through the heavy door connecting the lobby to the rest of the shelter. We step into a T-shaped corridor. The end of the long hallway houses the dog kennel, but Ms. Keely walks me up and down the short hall first.

"How long have you been director of the shelter?" I ask.

"For a little over a year now," she answers. "But before that, I volunteered here for quite some time. Since college."

College doesn't seem like that long ago for Ms. Keely. She looks about the same age as my oldest cousin, who is twenty-five.

She stops to peer through a door's glass window. "Say hi to our feline family," she says.

I stand next to her and wave to the two people handling and playing with the kitties inside. It's a large room furnished with all types of cat scratch posts and things for climbing.

"Aww, volunteering here would be a *dream*," I gush—though that came out more corny than I thought it would. Marie would roll her eyes at me if she were here, and Connor would tease me. But Ms. Keely isn't judging me for it. She only seems to get more animated by our conversation. So, I'm free to geek out to whatever level I wish.

"I'm sure you'll have no problem getting placed at a local shelter in a few years," she says. I wonder if *this* shelter will still be here when I'm old enough to volunteer. "Now, let me show you our kitchen."

We step into a narrow room with a sink on the left side and a long counter on the other.

"Nice!" I look around me.

This is such an organized little space. Piled up

high on top of the overhead counters are stacks of stainless steel doggy bowls. Ms. Keely opens up a lower cabinet and I help her store an open bag of dog food in there.

She then grabs a clean towel and wipes down the sprays of water on the counter. *I guess she's more than a director around here.* "How does it feel to manage a place where you've always volunteered?"

"It feels like home," she says. "I think by now I've done every job there is in this place, and I see how super important each role is. More and more, I'm grateful for the shopkeeping chores I had to

do during childhood visits to see my *lola* in the Philippines."

Once she tosses the towel in a laundry bin, we leave the room, pass the lobby door again, and head to the other end of the short hallway. The dogs in the kennel must sense Ms. Keely's presence, because they all start barking like crazy.

"Hello, friends!" she bellows out to them. I chuckle at the way they seem to reply in howling greeting. Now I'm extra eager to meet them at the end of the tour.

Ms. Keely is holding the door to a bigger room open for me. The door shuts behind us, muffling out the canine chorus.

"This is our grooming station slash medical exam room," Ms. Keely says proudly.

I can see why she's showing it off. The place looks super updated compared to the kitchen. There's even a new pet bathtub.

"We just got this place renovated, and all of it—the tub, the cabinets, the counters—was donated. Even the contractors donated their time to install everything."

"That's amazing!"

"Yup," says Ms. Keely. "It took a lot of knocking on doors, but the renovation and the medical care program are some of my crowning achievements since I became director. Now our furry friends can get examined and vaccinated here. I'm so grateful to the vets who take on rotating volunteer shifts."

"Very cool," I say. I'm in awe.

"I knew the shelter was having money problems when I started as director, but I didn't realize how bad the situation was until I dug deeper. I wanted to know exactly what I was dealing with so I could come up with a plan. And then the perfect storm hit when our hot water heating system broke down over the summer. The repairs cost us close to ten thousand dollars."

I shake my head, like *whoa*. For a moment, besides the occasional muffled bark, the only sound is the hum of a computer. Until Ms. Keely claps once, loudly. She starts rubbing her palms together as if she's got a special surprise.

"Hey, I know a few friendly creatures who would *love* to head out for a walk right now," she announces, a generous smile lifting her whole face.

"Let's do this," I say.

When we *finally* get to the kennel at the end of the long hallway, the dogs are even more excited than I am. On each side of the kennel hall are five roomy stalls fenced in with chain-link gates. Two handlers, a teen girl and boy, are clearing the farthest stalls of doggy bowls. Aware there are two new people nearby, the dogs in the other stalls rush to their gates in happy greeting. Some of them lean their front paws against their gates. Others try and poke their noses through its openings.

"Here I am, friends. Hi. Hi." Ms. Keely takes a few leashes off their hooks.

"Everyone say hi to Hope."

A perfectly timed response breaks out in the form of a short bark. It's coming from a dog near the back door at the end of the hall. Ms. Keely and I both crack up.

"He's a show-off, that Ralph," she says.

I head over to say hi to Ralph. A bright-eyed pit bull mix, he really does look like he speaks human. After giving me a once-over, Ralph grows bored with me. He scampers over to the chew toy in his woolly dog bed and busies himself with it.

"I think Baby would make the perfect walking

companion for you," Ms. Keely says, ushering a trio of leashed dogs toward me. She hands me the leash connected to a cute mutt with what looks like freshly shorn hair. "He's such a sweet little guy—super calm."

She's right. Baby stays in step with me during our walk. We follow the mulch path snaking through the spacious backyard until we reach the dog run. We arrive just as a man in a green Eastern Shore Animal Shelter tee is leaving with three more leashed rescues. We wave at one another in passing.

Baby and the two other dogs take off running when we unleash them in the dog run. Ms. Keely and I have a seat on a garden bench and watch them play.

After taking a few laps around the yard, Baby comes to the shade of our bench to get a drink of water from a doggy bowl there. It does feel extra hot, so I don't blame him for slowing down. I reach down and pet his head, and I watch his long rib cage rise and fall with his steadying breaths. He relaxes like he doesn't have a care in the world.

"What if everything we do to help the shelter doesn't make a dent?" I wonder aloud.

"Who's to say it doesn't make a dent?" Ms. Keely scooches to the end of the bench to give me a playful side eye, her head cocked away from me, and more wavy brown strands fall from her loose bun. "What's your favorite subject?" she asks.

"Science," I answer, lightning-quick.

"Well, then you must know what adding just a few drops of vinegar does to a baking soda–based solution."

"It bubbles up and smokes like an active volcano."

"That's right. Just a few drops." She wiggles her fingers.

I nod and smile at her passion for what she's saying.

The dog run gate clinks, and we're joined by an

older woman and Ralph, the talking dog. Even when she unclips Ralph's leash, he stays at the woman's side.

"Hey there." Ms. Keely gets up and shakes the guest's hand. "Ralph looks so happy you're back again."

"What can I say?" the woman says. She bends down to pet Ralph, and he licks her face before she can back away. "I think he's convinced me to take him home."

"Congratulations!" Ms. Keely whoops, excited. She balances on the balls of her feet the whole time she's speaking. "What a good-news afternoon this turned out to be. First Hope drops off funds raised from her doggy daycare fund-raiser, and now this."

"Wait, was this yesterday's dog-sitting by the beach?" Ralph's soon-to-be adoptive parent asks.

"Yes," I say.

"My friend Arnold dropped his dog, Frankie, there. He told me about you and your efforts. I came right over yesterday to see how I could help, and that's when I fell in love with Ralph here."

Like a reflex, a hand springs to my heart. "Wow," is all I can say.

Ms. Keely turns to wink at me. "And you made this happen. I told you. Just a few drops."

My cheeks hurt from smiling.

"Just a few drops," I repeat.

♡🐺☆

When four thirty rolls around, my mom is waiting for me outside the shelter as planned. By then, I've already made friends with the two other dogs in the dog run. There's Cocoa, the adorable chocolate Labrador mix with a weakness for a chew toy slathered in peanut butter. And a bashful boxer with three legs named Pixel who finally let me pet her on my way out.

"Thank you," Ms. Keely tells me in the lobby as she hands me my backpack.

I give Ms. Keely a hug goodbye, pumped I've already made more of a difference than I'd imagined.

"How did it go?" Mom asks the moment I step into her lemon-scented car. I take a nice big whiff.

"Great . . . ," I say, thinking of Ralph's new owner, before remembering the mountain of money the shelter needs. ". . . and not so great."

"How so?"

I tell Mom about how much Ms. Keely has to raise in such a short time.

"They're in worse shape than I thought," says Mom. She's filling her cheeks with air the way she does when she's trying to make up her mind. "But you'd be amazed what people and businesses can overcome in just a short time. Don't count them out."

I stare out the window at the palm trees and pedestrians swooshing by as we drive home. I check my phone and read all the group chat texts that have come in. Sam, Lacy, Camila, and Golda all want to help out with the adoption event Wednesday afternoon, but Charlie can't make it. Not surprisingly, neither can Grace. *Wonder what's up that she's so busy all the time.*

"She sounds like a lovely person, that Ms. Keely," says Mom, giving my free hand a squeeze. I look at her and smile.

"She is." I put down my phone. "Mom, you should see how much better the place looks now. So different from when we picked up Cosmo and Rocket."

"People like her care so deeply about what they're doing. I find that inspiring."

"Well, I can't stop now, Mom. Ralph is this super

smart dog at the shelter, and now he is getting adopted because of word of mouth that started with *my* doggy daycare by the beach."

"I wouldn't dream of you stopping," says Mom. "You're unstoppable."

Just like a Galaxite.

Don't count us out.

Chapter 6

The next day, I'm so overloaded with schoolwork, I don't get the chance to do any fund-raising planning for the shelter. After school in the library, as I'm finishing up my English essay, the thought hits me: It's time to reach out to the most creative thinkers I know. My family.

I text them right away. *Emergency family meeting after dinner.*

From that point, time seems to crawl, and my eagerness does nothing to make the time go by faster. After what feels like an eternity, the family meeting finally starts.

"What's up, sweetie?" Dad asks.

He and Mom are sitting across from me at our kitchen table. Marie is here, too. Well, more like *there*. She's a few feet away, leaning her elbows on the kitchen counter.

I shrug. "Help me brainstorm? We need to go ham on this final fund-raising weekend. Maybe we can plan a few events we can host or something."

"How about you think about the locations each person in your group has access to, and then brainstorm an event that would make sense for it," suggests my crafty mom.

"Aah, good thinking," says Dad, smiling.

"Dad, you've got something—" I gesture to him that there's spinach caught between his teeth. He does a tongue sweep.

"How about now?" he asks my mom, who gives him the all-clear thumbs-up.

Something furry brushes against my leg. Rocket's under the table looking for fallen scraps of food from our pasta dinner. Cosmo is at the foot of my chair, giving me strong pick-me-up vibes. One look at his pleading eyes and I give in. I pick him up and place him on my lap.

"I can name one person off the bat," I say, petting Cosmo. "Camila."

Mom nods and pushes away her empty glass. "Her family has the bakery."

"Yup," I say, scribbling down her name and the word "bakery." "Ooo! And last weekend, she gave me some homemade treats for the doggy daycare that looked so good, we were all tempted to have some. Maybe she can sell some to raise money for the shelter."

"I may have to actually try one of those treats," says Dad.

"Ew!" Mom, Marie, and I all squeal and crack up.

"Why not? It's just food," he says, shrugging.

Now what? I stare at the word "bakery" until the letters blur. That's when I see it.

"Hey, wouldn't it be cute if she could rename it a *barkery* for a fund-raising weekend?" I ask.

Dad smiles. "That's fun."

"I like it," says Mom. "But you need to make sure Camila's dad is willing to go along with this plan."

"I will," I say.

Marie sighs and walks over to the sink. The faucet is on full blast for a second, and we wait for her to shut it off before talking again.

"Well, there's your gallery space, of course," I tell Mom.

"I mean, hello!" Mom points to herself, pretending to be offended. "Thank you. I thought you'd never bring it up."

"What kind of events do you like to hold there?"

"Artist shows, auctions—and, oh, we've been doing more photography lately."

"What if we hold an auction of different donated prizes? That's what they're doing for the Fall Formal."

"I can easily donate tickets to the next rocket launch," offers Dad.

"Ohmygosh, that would be so cool!" I keep going back and forth between clapping excitedly to scribbling in my notebook as fast as possible.

"That settles it. We can hold the event next Wednesday night, say at five," says Mom, looking at the calendar app on her phone. I jot down the date and time in my notebook.

"Sounds perfect!" I shout.

The sharp clang of dishes disrupts my celebration. Marie is at the sink, piling up more plates and glasses from our meal.

"The dishwasher is already working on the first load," Mom tells her. "There's nowhere to put those until that's done."

I guess Marie would rather scrub everything by hand than join us in this brainstorming session.

She's acting like we forgot it's her birthday or something.

"So, Marie, what do you think?" Dad asks.

Marie finally walks to the table, but Rocket stops her halfway in greeting. Marie kneels down to pet her. "About what?"

"About what you can contribute."

I sigh. "Dad, I think she wants to stay out of the conversation. It's obvious she's not interested," I say.

"That's not true at all," says Marie, offended. "What makes you say that?"

"Um, maybe because you're walking around acting like one of those people who wears shades indoors."

"Maybe what's not interesting me are your ideas, not your goals."

"All right, you two," says Mom.

"Whoa," Dad says at the same time.

"But I do like the barkery idea and think you guys should keep the cute names coming. Like, Mom, you can call the gallery auction event a *Yappy* Hour."

I rapid-blink a few times, already envisioning it.

Marie isn't done. "And see if you can have someone take pics of the dogs being dogs. Kinda the way our family portrait has Dad being spinach-teeth Dad. With the dogs, they'll be lovable and funny images, so people can get to know the dogs' personalities."

"Wow, that's an amazing idea," I say. "Thank you."

"You're in the science club," Marie continues. "Why don't you ask a few of the members to set up a kennel cam or something? That way people can see the dogs' personalities some more, and hopefully donate or adopt one of them."

I scoot to the edge of my seat and shout, "I love that!"

"So good!" says Dad.

Marie does a single shoulder shrug and gives a half smile.

Mom looks proud of her two girls. "And Marie, you know lots of people and have so many followers from school online. What if you spread the word about tomorrow's adoption event?"

"Yeah, invite a few friends to the beach," suggests Dad. "We'll all be there."

Marie scrunches up her nose and chuckles. "Um, that's not a selling point."

"You've just earned your friends an extra dad joke." He playfully points at her.

"Let the record show that even with that scary threat, I'll still be there tomorrow," says Marie. She stops playing with Rocket and stands up.

"Time to turn over every stone and call in favors," Mom says. "That includes you, Hope."

"I reached out to all my friends already," I say, confused. "Almost all of them are coming."

"You can branch out further than your friends.

I'm sure there are other kids at JFK Middle who would be interested in helping the shelter."

Oh. I've been so much in my own bubble at school that I hadn't thought of that.

"I'll try my best," I say, lifting Cosmo's small paw and giving him a high five. "Thanks, fam jam."

I hug my parents, grab my phone and notebook, and head toward my bedroom. That's when I hear Marie whisper behind my back to my parents.

"Don't you think it's a bit irresponsible of you to encourage Hope to take this on when there's no way she'll meet the goal by next week?"

And then—*incoming!*—my mood tumbles back to solid ground, and my face falls along with it.

Chapter 7

"**H**ope Roberts, reporting for duty!" I shout over the sound of the ocean's frothy waves. It's a crowded afternoon at the beach, despite being a Wednesday. I'm with Marie and our crews of friends, and we're all super excited to find some dogs new homes.

"Hey!" says Ms. Keely, hopping off the pet adoption camper to meet everyone. We each give her a salute before she shakes our hands.

"These are my friends Sam, Camila, Lacy, and Golda. And this is my sister, Marie, and her friend Diya." No one else I was brave enough to ask—including Henry—was able to tag along so last minute.

"Thanks for coming." Ms. Keely shows them her trademark big smile. "With this many of you, setup will take no time!"

Mom and Dad have just finished walking Cosmo and Rocket. Our family pups try to run toward us when they see me, but my parents grip their leashes tighter.

"Hello, we're Hope's parents, Jessica and Chris," says Mom, smiling.

Ms. Keely does a little hop. "Pleased to meet you. And who do we have here?"

"These are our rescues, Cosmo and Rocket."

Ms. Keely pets them like they've just done something amazing, like doggy-surfed a gigantic wave.

"Looks like you've got all the helping hands you need," says Dad to Ms. Keely. "We'll keep walking the beach, spreading the word about adoption day."

"That's a huge help, thanks so much," she answers, smoothing back her hair, calming the strands blown loose by the whipping wind. "All right, team, let's get ready!"

In the next ten minutes, we unload card tables and folding chairs. It's too windy to leave out any adoption leaflets, but we arrange the shelter's tablets in a neat row.

The shelter employees build a fence that will corral the potential adoptees. They bring out the dogs, two by two. Almost right away, the eight dogs attract a group of people.

"Aww, Mommy, I want one!" says a little boy who runs up for a closer look.

"You're welcome to gently pet him," invites Ms. Keely.

Ms. Keely and two shelter employees charm people almost as much as the cute pups do. They answer every last question—and there are many of them—about the dogs while Marie and Diya dog-sit. Camila and I keep the dogs' water bowls filled and their area cleaned. Lacy, Sam, and Golda use their charisma to bring in the potential pet parents strolling by.

"You just have to meet these cuties. They'd

make a sweet addition to your family," I hear Lacy call out.

The dogs seem happy to be surfside, and they take special joy in barking at the other dogs walking by with their owners. I love seeing them not cooped up in a cage.

At the end of the three-hour event, the shelter got some new donations, more people learned about our cause, *and* two dogs have gone home with lucky families. I think of Ms. Keely's words: *Every drop counts.*

The new adoptees weren't dogs that I met during my visit, but Ms. Keely says they had been sheltered for more than six months! Witnessing a love connection between a pup and their new family is amazing. I'm even more pumped to do all I can to put my own plan into action.

Starting now.

♡🐺☆

After we help Ms. Keely pack up the camper and watch it pull off into the sun, Marie, Diya, my friends, and I gather on picnic blankets to celebrate and hang out. Mom and Dad drop off Cosmo and Rocket before heading to their dinner date.

"This was such a good idea, Hope," says Sam. "I'm glad you got us all out here."

I shoot my best friend a smile while I text Grace. She sent an apology for missing the event. When I ask her what she has been working on, a typing bubble with flashing dots pops onscreen before disappearing entirely. *Weird.*

"Wasn't it cool?" says Lacy, walking on her knees until she can reach for an apple from the picnic basket Dad and I prepared.

"I know—I totally didn't expect that to be as much fun as it was," says Camila. She pulls out baggies from her backpack.

"What are those?" Marie asks her from the neighboring blanket she's now sharing with Diya.

"I baked more doggy biscuits," says Camila. "I heard my last batch was a hit at the dog park."

"You sure you haven't tested them out on yourself first?" I ask with a sneaky smile. "They look hard to resist."

"A baker never reveals her secrets," Camila says, grinning.

"I thought that was a magician's line," I chuckle.

"You are so amazing at baking," says Lacy, who

never misses the chance to encourage or compliment someone.

Camila grins before tossing each dog a treat.

"Don't spoil them too much, or they won't want to come back home with me," I joke, reaching into the picnic basket for a snack of my own.

A flock of seagulls lands a little too close to our group. Cosmo and Rocket hurl enough threatening barks and gestures at the flock that they get the hint and clear the area.

At that moment, Rocket barks at an incoming bird, and it flies off before it even gets the chance to touch down.

We all burst out laughing at the bird's "never mind" decision.

"Aw, poor thing," says Lacy, who's failing at stifling her laughter.

While the girls are enjoying the turkey sandwiches my dad helped me prepare after school, I start talking.

"I'd love it if we could all work together on the Yappy Hour auction. We need to ask more people and businesses to donate items folks would love to bid on." I stress to my friends that this is the quickest way for us to raise the huge amount of money the shelter needs by next week.

Sam looks confused. "How much is twenty thousand dollars, even?"

"What do you mean?" Camila asks, trying to avoid Cosmo's and Rocket's pleading eyes. They obviously loved her homemade treats.

I know what Sam means, but I'm not sure how to explain it.

"Like, what costs that much money in life?" Sam asks.

"The most money I've heard my mom talk about

is the two thousand dollars for my theater camp," Lacy says.

"Just break the number down," says Golda, jumping into that magical tutoring mode Lacy's always raving about. "You can wrap your head around a one-hundred-dollar bill, right? Depending on where you shop, one hundred dollars can get you about three pairs of shoes."

We all nod.

Golda has put down her sandwich, and she makes eye contact with each of us as she teaches—er, talks. "Well, if you stack up two hundred of those bills, that equals twenty thousand dollars."

"That's a lot of shoes," I say, thinking of the collection in Marie's closet.

Golda is pointing at me now. "Now calculate how many pairs twenty thousand dollars could get you."

Camila is using the calculator on her phone as we envision all the cute footwear.

"That's, like, six hundred pairs of shoes."

"So . . . basically imagine buying six hundred pairs of shoes in nine days."

"That's kind of a bummer," says Marie. I hadn't realized she was paying attention to Golda's tutorial.

"Are you sure it's even worth trying at this point? I mean, what if all of your efforts are for nothing?"

"Why do you have to be such a hater, Marie?" I snap, afraid she's going to influence my friends not to help. Ever since she started high school, it's like Marie thinks she's too cool to get excited about anything.

"It's just a question she's tossing out, that's all," says Lacy the peacemaker. My jaw loosens and I stop gritting my teeth at Marie. "I have a good feeling about this. It's all going to work out for the best, whether you decide to fund-raise or not."

"We're *definitely* fund-raising. So . . . who's in?" I ask.

"Sam, we can go floor by floor in my mom's office

building, asking businesses to donate prizes for the auction," says Lacy, beaming.

"Let's do it in character!" Sam claps. "We'll promote our show *and* help the shelter—it's a win-win!"

"That's a good idea, Sam," says Camila. "With the Fall Formal dominating everything at school, I almost forgot about the musical."

"Hey, you should hit up the Fall Formal fundraisers, too," calls out Diya from the neighboring blanket. "They are good at asking people for money. Especially now that they've teamed up with the alumni people. I just graduated from JFK Middle, and my parents have been spammed with emails about donating to all of these alumni fund-raisers."

Sam bobs her head in agreement. "I heard we have alumni money to thank for the school's new pool."

"True, they still email my mom, and she graduated eons ago," I say.

"Plus, they've got a crowd-funding page set up on the alumni website, and it looks amazing," says Golda. "It's got a flashy video and a list of cool prizes for top donors."

"I wonder if the school would be open to linking to the shelter on their website, or letting donors have the option of sending a portion of their donation to the shelter instead," I say.

"It couldn't hurt to ask," says Camila.

My eye catches Marie's, but she looks away. She's petting Rocket, who has gone to sit with her, and pretending she didn't hear our brainstorming. Good. I'd rather have her ignore these ideas than ridicule them.

"I like it." I hop up to sit on my legs. "Teaming with Fall Formal people and tapping into that alumni fund-raising sounds like the moooove."

Rocket howls back like she's saying "moooove," too, and we all crack up hysterically.

Feeling more hopeful than ever, I laugh the loudest.

Galaxites to the *rescues*!

Chapter 8

"**A**ll I'm saying is twenty grand is a lot of money, and you don't have that much time," says Marie. "And what about the formal? Have you even thought about what you're going to wear? I said I'd help you find the perfect dress."

We're alone in the car for the few minutes it's taking my dad to pump gas, and Marie is already trying to distract me from my mission.

"Well, a fashion stylist is not the kind of assistance I need right now," I snap from the back seat.

"Don't get your curls in a twist. I said I'd do what I can for the shelter, too," she says.

"You call this helping? I know you don't think we can save the shelter."

"How are my girls?" Dad sticks his head through the open driver's side door. He either heard or sensed our bickering.

We both roll our eyes and don't answer.

"Good to know. Now say cheese!"

Dad snaps a pic of our pouty faces before we can take cover or look away. We both crack up in spite of our cranky attitudes.

"Aaah, that sounds more like it!" Dad grins, waving his arms and playing the conductor to the symphony of our laughter.

Sister squabble squashed . . . for now.

♡🐺☆

The first thing I do when I get to school is sign up to meet with the vice principal. I have a half hour before class, so I'm hoping she's available today.

Last night, after our postadoption event picnic, I checked out the JFK Middle alumni website. The girls were right: It is awesome looking. Bright, fun font, funny GIFs, and vivid photos of school events from the near and distant past, including the Fall Formal. Of course, Marie is looking fly in her eighth-grade Fall Formal photo from last year. And they even featured a pic of my mom from her own JFK Middle Fall Formal appearances. They both are styled like top models.

After poking around online for a few minutes, I found out that Ms. Reimer, the vice principal, is both an alumna and the faculty advisor for the Fall Formal. From studying the school handbook and hanging on to every word during orientation and assemblies, I know Ms. Reimer holds first-come-first-served office hours on some mornings.

Today, I'm the first name on the sign-up sheet.

"Do you know when Ms. Reimer is expected in?" I ask the man behind the huge front desk in the main office.

"She's here, but she's with a student right now," he says. "Take a seat and you'll be next."

There were no other names on the list. This must

be the scheduled-talk kind of office visit. *I wonder who it's with.*

After ten minutes of trying to figure out when I'll find time to find a Fall Formal outfit, looking at all the student campaign posters on the bulletin board, and going over the written fund-raising questions I have for Ms. Reimer, her office door opens.

Out rolls a girl in a wheelchair I've seen around the school before. I'm pretty sure she's a seventh grader, because she has a locker near Henry's. Not that I've searched for his locker—but I have noticed where it is.

"That's Grace for ya," Ms. Reimer is saying to the girl. "Top-notch work."

My ears perked when I heard Grace's name. But there are other Graces at JFK Middle, like the eighth grade's star soccer player. Either way, whoever they were talking about, the girl rolling toward me is grinning from ear to ear.

"Hey," I greet her when she passes by me.

"Hi there!" she says, extra sunny. It seems like her personality matches her outfit. She's wearing a lot of pink. Some of her blond hair is even sprayed pink. Then there's the sequins detailed on her denim vest and her tutu, which she wears over a pair of leggings. But surprisingly, her look isn't childish; it's actually rock-star cool.

She continues out of the office before I have a chance to introduce myself.

"Hope Roberts." The secretary reads my name off the list. "You can go in now."

"How can I help you?" Ms. Reimer asks as she walks me into her office.

I practiced my speech to her from a seated position, since I had envisioned we would be eye to eye, meeting minds across her desk. But I end up having to throw my words across the room, because she lingers behind me to water the plants lined next to her door.

I turn to face her, because studies show humans are more inclined to absorb and make a connection to an oral story if eye contact is established. But her back is to me, so no eye contact, either. Instead of

Ms. Reimer's brown eyes, all I have is the back of her brown suit jacket.

"Go on, I'm listening," she says, and I can't help but wonder if she's talking to me or her plants.

"Well, our town is a little more than a week away from losing the longest-running animal rescue in this county. The Eastern Shore Animal Shelter will shut down if twenty thousand dollars can't be raised before next Friday's deadline. Since JFK Middle is so successful at hosting charitable events to raise money for the school, I was wondering if we could do something to support the shelter, too. We can highlight what they're going through. And when alumni and families go to the school's website, we can give them the option of donating to the shelter as well as the school."

"The website isn't really my territory, and quite frankly, it's out of my field of expertise," says Ms. Reimer's brown jacket. "But I'm a sucker for rescues. I've had a few of them over the years myself."

Ms. Reimer finally puts down the watering can. Relieved, I rub the ache in my neck I now have from twisting to talk to her. I face forward for a few long seconds, but Ms. Reimer still doesn't take the seat across from me. When I turn around again, she's tidying up the rear seating area: plumping the small couch pillows and rearranging their placement. The floral patterns with the floral patterns. The plaid print with the plaid print.

"I'll tell you what I'll do. I'll connect you with the head of the Fall Formal planning committee. That girl is a star. You can learn a lot about fund-raising from her."

"But, Ms. Reimer, the shelter doesn't have much time—"

"If you'll hold on, I'll get to that. Now, do you think I should mix the plaid with the floral or leave the pillows like this?"

Huh? I twist my neck again, because my chair's high armrests stop me from turning my body around for a better look.

"It looks nice as it is," I say as thoughtfully as possible, even though I honestly don't have an opinion on her décor.

"Remind me not to put you on the decorating committee," chuckles Ms. Reimer as she mixes up the pillows so the patterns clash.

"Ask one of the Fall Formal volunteers to introduce

you to the head of the planning committee. She'll help you set up the link to your fund-raising page and add an option for donors to give to the shelter."

"Who is the head of the—?"

"Good luck with the shelter. Goodbye for now," Ms. Reimer says with full eye contact. Finally.

She walks over to her door and holds it open for me to walk through.

"Thank you," I say gratefully as I exit her office. Once I'm in the hallway I pull out my notebook and cross off *Ask for Website Donation Button*. Next task? *Find Fall Formal Volunteer*, I scribble.

We're making progress, but my checklist doesn't

seem to be getting any shorter—and there's only eight days left.

♡🐺☆

Of course, today of all days, there's not one bake sale or sign-up table for the Fall Formal set up anywhere.

Ugh. I want to bang my head against my locker, but instead, I open it and stare at everything inside like it's a fridge and I'm deciding what to eat. After grabbing a few textbooks, I close it with a loud sigh.

All morning, I keep an eye out for the Fall Formal volunteers, but their wall-to-wall tables seem to have disappeared from school. With the dance next week, they've probably secured all the volunteers they need and sold all the advanced

tickets. It isn't until lunch that I finally spot one of their tables in the cafeteria.

"I'll be right over," I say to my lunch buddies, Grace and Camila. Sam has a different schedule, so we don't eat at the same time. Even though I miss my best friend, lunch with Grace and Camila has become a fun time.

"We'll save you a seat," says Grace, pushing her glasses up her nose. Her bangs now perfectly swoop over her glasses. *With her schedule being so busy lately, I'm surprised Grace found time for a haircut.*

"Thanks!" I say. "I'll be right back."

I trot over to the small table like I'm crossing a busy street. As I get closer, I totally recognize the

volunteer there. It's the sparkly rocker girl from outside Ms. Reimer's office.

She calls out to me even before I get to the table.

"Hey there!"

"Hi." I smile back, closing the gap between us.

"It's a great day to buy dance tickets or sign up for a committee," she says.

"Uh, not right now," I say, not nearly as bubbly. "I just have a question. I wonder if you can tell me who the head of your planning committee is? Ms. Reimer wants me to work with her on a fund-raising project."

"Sounds about right. Ms. Reimer can't stop raving about her 'attention to detail,'" the girl says, smiling, raising her fingers, and framing air quotes.

"So . . . do you know where I can find her?"

She shoots me a confused look. "I just saw you walk in with her."

"What? I did?"

She nods with a warm smile. "And, by the way, I can tell she just got her hair trimmed and I love it."

This planning committee genius is . . . *Grace*?

Chapter 9

Who knew Grace was even *into* the formal? Camila has been constantly harping on it at lunch and in the hallways and at science club. She's over the eager volunteers; plus, she thinks everyone else is too excited about the whole thing. *Is that why Grace never told us she's playing a major role in the event?*

I turn around to look at Grace. Camila is chatting away, pointing at me every few seconds. Grace is craning her neck to get a visual of me. She's quietly listening to what I assume is Camila telling her about my new Rescue the Rescues mission.

"Thanks for your help," I tell the volunteer.

"Anytime!" she answers with a wave.

"Camila just told me about your plan," Grace says as I sit down next to her.

I don't want to bring up a subject that's uncomfortable for Grace to discuss in front of Camila, so I just nod my head.

"You texted this morning before you met with the vice principal, but you haven't told me what happened," says Camila between bites of her lunch.

I can't mention Ms. Reimer geeking out over Grace.

"It went well," I say as casually as possible.

Camila studies my face, waiting for more details, but they don't come.

"And?" she asks.

"And . . . she agreed to add a donation link to the school's website. And she wants me to work with the Fall Formal planning person," I say.

Grace toys with her pasta dish, but she doesn't bring another bite to her mouth. She catches my eye, and then looks back at her food.

"Was that the girl you just talked to over there?" Camila peers around me to eye the girl at the Fall Formal table.

Who knew Camila could talk about the Fall Formal for this long without getting worked up or having bridezilla flashbacks? She actually sounds interested.

"Uh—not exactly," I respond.

Grace puts down her lunch and starts wringing her fingers.

Like we're in a tennis match, Camila looks suspiciously at Grace, then at me, then back to Grace again.

"What aren't you telling me?" Camila asks us, confused.

"Okay, okay," Grace says. She moves aside her bowl of noodles and rests her bare elbows on the table. Her plump cheeks are tinged with red. "I have a confession to make."

I sigh with relief.

"Grace, you know there's no judgment here," I say, hoping Camila gets the hint not to make this hard for her.

Grace nods. "The reason I've been too busy to come with you to the shelter or the adoption event is because I've been helping out with the Fall Formal. Like, a lot."

Camila gasps. *"You?"*

"Why is it so shocking that someone like me would do this?" Grace asks through her frown.

"Grace, that's great!" I say, hoping to distract my lunch buddies from going at it.

Maybe I should do a magic trick.

"Aw, I didn't mean it to sound like that," Camila says apologetically. "It's just you never talk about it."

"I guess I was afraid of getting trolled for it," Grace says, a little embarrassed.

"By me?" Camila asks innocently, batting her eyelids for extra effect. "Why would I do something like that?"

"Yeah," I say, wagging a finger in the air. "Shame on you for thinking Camila's the type to trash the Fall Formal."

Grace laughs with her hand on her chest. Her eyes gleam with happy relief.

"My bad," she says.

Camila grins. "Anyway, I know you're not the type to let the Fall Formal turn you into a total overdemanding dancezilla."

"Does that mean you'll come?" Grace asks, and I almost hold my breath waiting for Camila's answer.

"Of course," she says, like it's common knowledge. "I already bought my ticket!"

"Huh?" Grace and I shake our heads at our friend and crack up. Camila bounces her shoulders, tickled she had us stumped.

"As Sam would say, it's a win-win," Camila explains. "I get to support a school cause *and* get dressed up to hang out with my friends."

"So, Grace," I say, scooting to the edge of my seat. "If this donation button plan sounds okay to you, when can we get started?"

"Yay, my very own intern!" She joins Camila in the shoulder bounce. "I have a cool place where we can meet after school."

♡🐺☆

As soon as the dismissal bell rings, I report to my unofficial internship. Thanks to her personal cheerleader, Ms. Reimer, Grace has after-hours access to the teachers' lounge. It's nice and comfy in there, with sunlight streaming in through large windows. This school's got a thing for couches with lots of pillows. There are even jewel-toned throw pillows over a cozy rug in one nook, and your seating choice of the couch or old-fashioned wooden chairs tucked into three matching round tables.

"This is nice," I tell her once I've couch-dived into the spot next to her.

"Just don't fall asleep." She grins. "Because I'm pretty sure that's what my social studies teacher does in here. She's always yawning, setting the entire class off."

I drop my head and pretend I'm dozing off the second Grace cracks open her laptop to show me her files.

"Hey!" she whines.

I laugh. "I'm only kidding. I actually can't wait to see what you've got!"

"And I can't wait to share!" She rubs her palms together. "It's been tough not talking about it."

"I'm sorry you felt like you had to hide it." I frown.

Creak.

We look to the door, which is now ajar.

"Maybe it's just the wind," I say, creeped out.

"Come on in, Bella!" Grace calls out.

The door swings open and the tutu-wearing rocker girl I saw outside Ms. Reimer's office and at the Fall Formal table rolls in. She parks her wheelchair facing the couch Grace and I are sharing.

"Hi there!" she says in the same friendly way she did the first time I saw her.

"You've already met my secret weapon, Bella Vreeland," says Grace. "She's saving the formal from all things tacky. She's like our decorator, designer, and diva all rolled up in one."

"Well, maybe not diva," Bella says with a chuckle.

"Facts," agrees Grace. "I just added that because I *thought* it sounded cool. You see why I should leave these things up to her?"

"Well, nice to officially meet you, Bella," I say, excited to meet another chill JFK Middle student. We need to stick together, because it's a jungle out there. Like, literally. There's a ginormous statue of a tooth-baring tiger in the school's main hall. "I'm Hope Roberts."

"Hi, Hope Roberts! Hey—are you related to Marie Roberts, who graduated JFK Middle last year?"

"Yes, that's my sister."

"Is she really? Ohmygosh, she is like *the* fashion

goddess. And she's super sweet, too. I so looked up to her. When she designed the costumes for last year's school musical, I *died*."

Huh? My sister *was the costume designer?* How did I miss that? I thought she'd just helped out with the sewing.

I keep waiting for Bella to take a breath, but she keeps the praise going strong. "You are so lucky to have Marie as a sister. Imagine being that close to her *closet*. She makes her own stuff, too. Her fashion tees are, like, my favorite."

But it's just as awkward when she stops talking, because I don't come up with anything to fill the sudden silence. I mean, what can I say? Confess that I wish I paid more attention to my sister? I swallow down the urge to blurt this out.

"Yeah," is all I say instead.

Grace picks up on the awkwardness, and she pulls back down her one stray eyebrow that seemed to go missing in her bangs while Bella was fangirling over my sister.

"Ahem—um, let's grab a table," Grace says as cheerily as possible.

At the table—we choose the center one—we all sit close enough to share Grace's laptop screen. Once I see her desktop, it's confirmed: The girl is neat about everything. I noticed it before in the way she neatly stacks her books and pens on her desk in class. But now, looking at her screen, seeing all the documents arranged neatly and her emails in labeled files, I'm impressed.

And every journal, pen, and notebook Bella pulls from her backpack says something about her style, too. She and Grace care so much about the details; I can see why they make a great team.

"This is my main spreadsheet." Grace points to a grid with labeled columns and rows. "Here's where I assign volunteer duties for the Fall Formal and keep track of what everyone is doing and when. This one here is my alumni donation document. I'm also keeping track of all the prizes we've lined up as giveaways for the alumni fund-raiser that's happening online."

I smile and give her a playful shoulder bump.

"What? Creating spreadsheets and making charts are hobbies of mine."

"Uh, it's a little more than a hobby. This is your superpower," I say with a grin.

She wrinkles her nose. "I admit, sometimes I go a little overboard. You'd be surprised what charts I have to force myself to delete. I have too many."

"You should see how many pairs of earrings I have to force myself to give away," says Bella. "At least your clutter is digital. It's hard to be a low-key hoarder IRL."

Bella makes the frazzled emoji face, and we share a good chuckle before kicking off our fund-raiser chat.

Once Grace starts talking, she just keeps it going. *How long has she been bottling up her feelings?* I'm glad it's all spilling out now. She's so good at this.

Over the next hour, I watch Grace's superpower in action. She helps me create a spreadsheet that will track all the fund-raising money and where it's coming from. There are categories for dog-sitting, Camila's barkery treats, auction items, and general cash donations. And it's all neatly listed in columns.

Next, we create Yappy Hour digital posters. People can email, text, or post them to share the time and location of the event next Wednesday.

Grace and Bella really do make a great superhero duo. When we move on to work on the website, everything Grace adds, changes, or rearranges is then redesigned by Bella, so she can make sure everything has a cool look, color, and feel to it.

We add the shelter link and the donation buttons to the school's home page. I come up with silly puns—corny stuff like "Reach into your PURRse and donate." Grace playfully rolls her eyes each time I come up with another one. Bella, though, cracks up.

"I like your style," says Bella, grinning. "I think that vibe works for the shelter."

"Then, watch me *werk* it," I say, doing the shoulder dance to Grace and Bella's squeals and laughter.

Chapter 10

Marie walks to the kitchen table with a plate of eggs and takes a seat across from me. With Mom still upstairs getting ready, and Dad already on his way to work, it's just the two of us. We sit in silence, listening to the chirping birds out our window. The occasional clinks of our

silverware add percussion to their songs.

Ever since the school year started, it's been less common for Marie and me to have breakfast together. She's on a different schedule, and she's been busy with her new high school life. Plus, for the past few mornings, she's had her nose in her sewing machine. Is she making costumes for her *high school* musical now?

But who am I to know what she's up to? I'm just her only sibling.

Maybe I should ask Bella. The girl probably has Marie's fashion résumé memorized . . . if there is one. I shrug to myself. And then I wince.

"Ouch, that was my foot!" I look under the table to find the culprit.

Cosmo and Rocket are so tangled up in their roughhousing, I can't say for sure who pawed me. Marie coughs out a chuckle. *Is she laughing at me?*

"So, I met the president of the Marie Fan Club yesterday," I say, cutting off her snickering.

"Who?"

"Are there that many presidential candidates?" I tease.

Marie stops chewing to give me a dead stare.

"Fine. Bella Vreeland. Sound familiar?" If it doesn't, I'd never have the heart to tell Bella.

But Marie's face lights up. Her smile even exposes her teeth.

"Aw, that's my girl—she's so talented. Tell her I said hi."

"Oh, I will." I look squarely at Marie. The morning sun lights the curves of her face like a lamp. "It's nice you don't think it's irresponsible to encourage *Bella* to meet *her* goals."

Marie cocks her head to the side, where it's shaded. "What does that even mean?"

"I heard you tell Mom and Dad they shouldn't support me in the shelter's fund-raiser."

"C'mon, Hope." She looks concerned. "You know I didn't mean it like that. I'm just looking out for you."

"Right," I say, rolling my eyes. "It sounds like that's what you do for *Bella*, not me."

Marie's face is back in the sun, her brown eyes like flickering flames. "Stop being such a brat and leave Bella out of this."

"Exactly like that," I snap. "Good lookin' out!"

My sister sits there seething but doesn't say a word.

The sound of our mom's chunky heels pounding the hallway approaches. In the next second, a blur of black, brown, and red blows into the kitchen and then back out again. I just catch the back of her flowy summer dress as she breezes through.

"Whoever's coming, let's go," Mom says on her way to the garage.

I grab a container and take my breakfast to go.

♡🐺☆

I'm counting on my next meal break to be drama-free. The vibe in JFK Middle's cafeteria is extra chill, so I'm sure it will be. I sit at our table and crack open my laptop, ready to show Grace how her spreadsheet is working for the shelter.

Grace set up a shared file for me and Ms. Keely where we can leave notes and updates for each other. So far, Ms. Keely is excited about our progress on Mission: Rescue the Rescues. She loves the barkery idea and can't get enough of my silly puns on the website. The kennel cam idea is her favorite. And thanks to the shelter link on the alumni website, Ms. Keely says the shelter has been getting a lot more online traffic.

Grace and Camila give me high fives when they see the spreadsheet. The latest update: Sam and Lacy's door-to-door canvass at the huge office building where Lacy's mom works has scored a ton of cool donated prizes for the Yappy Hour! So far, in the column marked *Auction Items*, I've listed Dad's rocket launch tickets, plus a laptop, concert tickets, and spa passes Sam and Lacy collected from donors. The tally for the total raised is at $875, including the doggy daycare money.

"And that number is rising every day," I tell them.

"Thanks in part to Camila's yummy dog treats," says Grace.

"How would you know how yummy they are?" I tease, and we all chuckle.

Camila turns to me. "Wait 'til you see my dog treats setup when you come by the bakery today."

"Can't wait!" I say. I'll be swinging by the bakery after school before I go to the shelter. The thought of seeing Ms. Keely—and all the dogs—again makes me clap like a baby seal.

"Thank you, thank you," Connor says, bowing to my mini applause as he and Shep walk by our table. "I know, I'm amazing."

A goofy grin stretches across Shep's face. They continue to their seats a few tables away.

Grace and Camila roll their eyes and keep chatting. But I suddenly hear my mom's voice in my head. *Call in favors.* There's one more awkward thing on my list I've been avoiding. I take a deep breath. *It's now or never.*

"Excuse me, girls," I say with an even tone. I'm clear-eyed, so I want to act on this now. If I wait, I may talk myself out of it.

I walk over to Connor's table. Shep is across from him, but he is in another world at the moment. Literally. He's reading a fantasy graphic novel I recognize.

"Hey," I greet Connor.

Connor is busy staring at his cell phone, pretending not to notice I'm there. *Please. No one texts that fast. Unless they're intentionally writing gibberish to be ironic.*

Time to use my old experiment. I clear my throat before speaking. "Connor, would it be better if I shouted, because I can shout if you can't hear me," I say sharply. Connor's phone slips through his stunned fingers and clatters to the tabletop. He leans back in his chair and stares at me like an ant would the underside of a shoe.

"Chill," I tell him. "I'm not gonna squish you."

"Huh?"

"Uh, never mind," I say, because to explain would be too weird.

"What do you want?"

"You've probably heard that a group of us are fund-raising to keep the Eastern Shore Animal Shelter from shutting down. Can I sign up you and Shep to help?"

Connor must forget to keep acting intimidated, because his face contorts into his trademark not-impressed scowl. He holds his mouth to one side of his face and gives me a laser-beam stare. "Why should I help you?"

"Don't look at it as helping me, but helping the animals."

His face stays frozen in that one expression. "Why should I help the animals?"

I get annoyed. "Well, maybe because it's the right thing to do; maybe because it qualifies you for community service points. Shall I go on?"

Connor's mouth slides back to its home above his chin. He looks nervously around the cafeteria, probably having flashbacks of my regrettable callout weeks ago. I can tell he doesn't want to risk me saying the wrong thing in public again.

"No pressure, of course." I soften at the memory. I don't want to feel like I'm strong-arming anyone to volunteer. That wouldn't be right. I'm taking a step back toward my table when Connor speaks up.

"What do I have to do?"

"I'd love it if you and Shep—and maybe the other guys in science club, too—could figure out how to rig a kennel cam for the shelter. We want to share a link to it on the website. If we're lucky it'll go viral, but at the very least it should help spread awareness—"

"Fine."

"Thanks. Our supply box from the science competition should have what you need," I say. "Oh, and can you guys work on it during today's science club meeting so we can go live this weekend?"

I take Connor's shrug as a yes.

Yay! It feels good to have one more major thing to cross off my checklist.

Chapter 11

Science club has been a lot less tense since the group project competition. In fact, today Mr. Gillespie dismisses everyone earlier than usual. Connor, Shep, and I stay to work on the kennel cam a little longer. Henry sticks around, too. He's hard at work, rigging a prop for the musical.

I wave to Grace on her way out the door. "Tell Bella I said hi."

"You got this," she answers with a nod at our project in process.

"So do you," I remind her, even though it's obvious Grace isn't worried. The Fall Formal is just a week away, and she's super chill about it. Camila has been proud of her for keeping a cool head under pressure.

"Catch you in a bit," I say to Camila as she heads to her family bakery.

She flashes me a smile. "See ya, Hope!"

"Are you done with the goodbyes?" Connor hisses at me. "I need quiet—I'm performing surgery here!"

Shep cackles out loud. Connor glares at him, and Shep's laughter shrinks to a smirk.

Connor turns back to his "patient" one last time. He uses the tweezers and finally pries the camera lens from the mini robot's belly. It only takes us a few more minutes to program the camera, and then we're done.

"Thanks, guys," I say, grateful.

"Glad to help the rescues," says Shep.

I carefully pack everything into my bag. "I'm going to the shelter today to set this up. Don't forget to tune into the livestream this weekend!"

"Cool," says Connor. He sounds surprisingly interested, but I have bigger things to worry about than whether or not Connor has something sneaky up his jacket sleeves. I have dogs to save, and only one week to do it.

"Goodbye, Connor! Goodbye, Shep!" I call at their backs in my sappiest voice as they walk out of the science lab.

Connor shakes his head. Shep smirks but doesn't risk laughing out loud.

Satisfied with myself, I grin.

"Wassup, Hope?" Henry is at my workstation when I turn back around. He's carrying the small prop he'd been working on.

"Hi," I say, clumsily finding a way to change my

goofy grin to a pleasant smile. I'm not sure I'm pulling it off, because my face feels fixed in a dopey grimace. *Help!*

I point to the prop he's carrying with both hands. "Let me guess—is that supposed to be an old-fashioned TV?"

"Close. It's supposed to be a fire-breathing wolf," he laughs.

"Oh, I almost had it," I chuckle. *Whew. Crisis averted.*

"Did I overhear you saying you're installing the kennel cam today?"

I nod.

"I can help you with that," Henry says, keeping pace with me as I slowly head for the exit.

"You mean like right now?"

"Uh-huh." Henry steps out in front of me to get the door. He uses his elbow to unlatch the door handle and his foot to pin open the door.

"Um," I say, barely able to glance at his face. He's looking at me, waiting for my reply. But if he comes, that'll sort of be like hanging out. After school. I'm only used to seeing Henry *at* school. For like an hour a week, at the most. What if

After-School Henry is a much different person than Science Club Henry?

"Okay, thanks. But first I need to meet Sam at the auditorium."

"That works," he says. "I need to drop this off there." He gestures to the prop.

"And then Sam and I need to swing by Camila's family bakery on the way," I explain, wanting to be clear about our plans. I bite my lower lip.

He nods. "Cool."

Welp, I guess After-School Henry is just as easygoing.

"Hey." A boy no taller than I am greets Henry by holding his hand like he 100 percent expects him to shake it. Henry doesn't leave him hanging, and they do an elaborate double backhand slap, side fist bump, and snap. The papier-mâché wolf Henry is carrying almost topples over. I grab one side to keep it steady.

"I've decided to run for student council vice president," the boy announces to Henry. "I hope I have your vote."

"Congrats, dude."

The boy continues walking, and Henry and I

move a few paces, too, before I realize I'm still carrying one end of the prop. It totally reminds me of the
time Henry helped me carry our science club robot
down this same hall. I glance at his smiling profile,
and wonder if he's thinking of the same memory.
As soon as I look away, he glances at me, and his
shoulder accidentally bumps against mine. I try my
best to hide my smile.

I shift the prop back into Henry's grip right before
we enter the auditorium. A teacher standing onstage
spots us right away.

"Is it ready, Henry?" she calls out.

"Yup! I'll bring it now," he answers, before turning to me. "If I see Sam, I'll tell her you're waiting."

"Thanks," I say, taking a seat.

I've just started leafing through my ideas notebook when Sam is standing above me, grinning.

"Henry said you guys talked and that he's coming with us." She winks. Sam has picked on my Henry crush before—not that I have confirmed that I have one. And with the way she's acting, I won't ever.

"So?"

"So . . . has he mentioned his friend Archie?"

"Who?"

"You know." Sam seems offended. "My crush!"

Sam quietly gasps and gestures to the stage with her head as discreetly as possible. A ginger-haired boy who looks like he was born with a paintbrush in his hand sees us and waves. Sam calmly waves back.

"Is that him?" I whisper.

Sam's eyes bug out in terror. "Shhh! I don't want my castmates to know."

"Okay, okay," I say.

"Ready to go?" It's Henry jogging up behind us, his gym bag flapping at his side.

Sam gives me a secret smile.

"Sure," she says, because my tongue is suddenly tied.

♡🐺☆

After we leave the school, we make a quick stop at Camila's family bakery, four blocks from JFK Middle, to check out the dog treat display.

"Hey, Hope! What's up, Sam, Henry?" Camila calls out to us as soon as we step into the yummy-smelling store. There are a few people having coffee and dessert at the small round tables sprinkled throughout the space. Soft rock music is faintly playing in the background.

"Camila, hey!" we greet her. We wave to her

dad, who is at one of the tables, showing his cake catalog to a young couple. He smiles and waves back.

Camila is behind the counter, beaming. The bright apron she's wearing goes perfectly with her mood. She points out the super cute display of doggy treats on the counter under a little sign that says BOW*WOW*! BARKERY—MADE FOR YOUR PUP and a few words about why we are raising money.

"Ooo!" Sam and I croon.

"Nice!" says Henry.

Sam takes a few pics of the doggy treat display for our website.

"And that's not all, guys!" says Camila. "My dad is all in for the barkery fund-raising weekend," she says.

I squeal like I've been poked in the belly. "Yes!"

"That's awesome!" says Sam, turning to give Camila's dad a thumbs-up.

Henry smiles, but it's mostly at the tasty cookies behind the display glass.

Camila nods and bounces on her toes. "He's donated enough ingredients for me to make dozens of dog treat baggies to sell here and at the auction.

Ooo, and we're putting out a donation jar for the shelter at the register. Plus, he's donating one free baking class for your Yappy Hour auction!"

"That's awesome!" I say. Next, I turn and call out to her dad. "Thank you so much, Mr. Rivera!"

I know he's in a meeting, but it's like a reflex I can't hold back. Mr. Rivera chuckles and answers that he is glad to help. The engaged couple sitting with him smile politely at me.

"Uh—we're going to the shelter now so Sam can take photos of the dogs," I tell Camila, figuring I've made enough of a scene here. "I'll send you a super cute one your dad can put with that donation jar."

Camila sends us off with a high five and a small box of free cupcakes to eat on our walk, plus a bag of dog treats to share with the pups at the shelter.

I feel lucky that I have so many great friends who are helping me rescue the rescues.

I just hope that everything we're doing is enough.

Chapter 12

When we get to the shelter, Ms. Keely is in the lobby, talking to a visitor. Her high bun looks even looser than last time. Henry, Sam, and I have our own conversation while we patiently wait for Ms. Keely to finish hers. Sam did most of the talking on our way here, and she's still talking to Henry now. I never have trouble talking to Science Club Henry at our meetings. We even worked closely together building the amusement park for the science competition. But this is different.

"Thanks again for coming with us, Henry," says Sam.

"Yeah, we really appreciate it, Henry," I say.

"It's no problem." He smiles at me. "My parents were just happy that I'm volunteering for the first time this school year."

When the visitor she'd been talking to leaves, Ms. Keely comes from around the counter to us.

"Hope! Sam! Good to see you again." Ms. Keely greets us with a hug. "And you brought a friend."

"Yes, this is Henry. He's in the science club with me. He's going to install the kennel cam I emailed you about."

"Well, welcome." She shakes his hand. "Sam, let's go meet your doggy models. They're playing in the dog run right now."

"Oh, then it's the perfect time for Henry to install the cam," I say.

"Yup, the kennel is pretty quiet at the moment," agrees Ms. Keely.

"Awesome." Henry nods, already in science project mode. On our way past the kennel, Ms. Keely leaves Henry with another volunteer so he can get to it.

Outside, I recognize Cocoa, Baby, and the bashful boxer running around. They seem to remember me, too, because they crowd me when I step into the gate.

"Hi, guys!" I crack up, petting them once they've calmed down.

"As for Ralph, he's thriving in his new home." Ms. Keely grins.

"Good ol' talking Ralph," I say happily.

"Let's see if he ever writes or calls me again."

"Don't hold your breath," I say, chuckling along with Ms. Keely.

After letting the dogs sniff her hand, Sam starts setting up her fancy camera. Her dad bought it for

her when he was moving to Ohio as a way for them to stay connected.

"Do you have any toys we can use as props?" Sam asks Ms. Keely.

"Sure, I'll have someone show you."

Ms. Keely walks over to the teen girl overseeing the dog run, and she leads Sam back inside the shelter.

"You guys make the future look so bright," says Ms. Keely when she joins me again. I'm back to tossing sticks for the playing dogs.

I smile and watch Cocoa bring me back the stick before I toss it again. "Hope, I've appreciated you keeping me updated on this awesome mission you're on," says Ms. Keely. "Now, *I* have an update to share with *you*."

I get excited. "Is the shelter staying open?"

"No, but our chances for staying open can be pretty much guaranteed if we get advance funding from the county," she explains.

"The county, as in the county we live in?"

Ms. Keely nods. She's also wringing her hands like they're made of sponge. "Every county in the state has its own seat of government. Several social programs are supported by the county, and this shelter is one of them. Every year they vote on whether to continue funding the shelter, and every year, it passes."

I wouldn't be surprised if water leaks from Ms. Keely's fingers.

"When is the next vote?"

She winces. "Well, it was supposed to be at the end of this year, which wouldn't help us, even if they did vote yes."

"Aw," I say, hanging my head.

"But I put together a proposal asking them to consider an earlier vote. I informed them about all the major improvements we've made since I became director. I also told them what a hit we took when we lost our biggest donor."

"And?" I say. If I had a tail, it would be wagging right now.

Ms. Keely flaps her hands like she's trying to take flight. "They agreed to an earlier vote!"

We high-five and stomp our feet.

"That's so great! Congratulations!"

"They're not happy with the financial mess the shelter is in, so there's no guarantee we'll get the green light." She bunches up her lips and crinkles her nose.

"But if they vote yes?"

"Well, then we are covered to stay open for at

least another six months to a year."

I let out a sigh of relief.

"But, if they *don't* fund us, it's pretty much the last nail in our coffin," she says. "Prepare yourself for that news."

"Is there anything we can do to convince them to vote yes?"

"Well, I plan on attending the county meeting where the vote will happen on Monday night. And I'm inviting anyone from the community who can come to join me."

"I'll be there!" I say before she even asks.

"I had a feeling you would be." Ms. Keely smiles that kindergarten teacher smile again. "And win or lose, after the vote, we're all meeting back here at the shelter to either celebrate or have a farewell gathering."

"I'm hoping with all my heart it'll be to celebrate," I say. Ms. Keely smiles her sad smile and I nod at her with confidence.

Then Sam is back with a huge bag of colorful toys and

props. "Let's get started!" she says.

Sam and I spring into action. We use the toys to wrangle the dogs into the camera's view.

A chew toy lands in a small puddle formed by today's rain. Cocoa goes for it, getting paw deep in muddy water and splashing it everywhere.

Click!

Sam captures the messy moment.

We throw a knotted dog rope onto the grass. Both a terrier mix and Pixel the boxer try to claim it. They grab either end and start a tug-of-war, pulling each other this way and that. Pixel holds her own, even with her missing front leg.

Click!

Baby is having another lazy moment in the shade. He stretches on his side, and then turns belly up with his jaw wide open in a yawn.

Click!

Fifteen minutes later, Sam checks her camera screen. "I think we've got it!"

Ms. Keely cheers and—what the heck—we join in with her.

Henry's setup complete, he meets us outside just in time to celebrate.

"These little guys were fun to hang out with," says Henry, face beaming while he scratches Cocoa's face. "They'll be fun to watch online, too."

"The livestream may help get the rest of our friends adopted, so we're grateful for it," says Ms. Keely.

Our deadline is creeping closer, but today was a good day. Maybe I can make posters using the photos we took for the town hall meeting. If I work on them all weekend, they'll be ready. And I'll be ready, too.

Chapter 13

Saturday morning, I take a break from poster making and head to Marie's room to return a jacket I "borrowed" from her. Something cobalt blue hanging deeper in her closet catches my eye, and I immediately think of the Fall Formal. It's this week, and I've been too busy with the shelter to figure out what I'm going to wear.

I know, it's an annoying kid sister thing to do, but I reach back in the closet and pull out the skirt that caught my eye.

I jump and whip around when I hear someone walk into her room.

Whew!

"Cosmo and Rocket, you guys scared me!" I playfully scold them. "I thought you guys were in the kitchen snacking."

Their tongues wipe the crumbs from around their mouths. Obviously they've finished.

The coast clear, I go back to nosing around. Marie and I have an unspoken understanding. As long as she doesn't catch me taking her clothes, I can wear them. I've noticed the secret looks of approval I get from her when she likes how I've styled her pieces with mine, especially some of the ones she's made herself.

"Sweet color," I say, holding the skirt to my front. It looks nice against my brown skin. "Think this would look cute for the formal, guys?"

Rocket and Cosmo respond by flopping onto the floor next to my feet.

"I know just what Marie would wear with this," I say to myself. "Tons of makeup."

Marie's vanity is crowded with all types of fun lipsticks, eye shadows, bronzers, and other products I don't know the names of. I'm not into that kind of stuff, but I love the colors.

"I wonder what this tube is for." When in doubt, try it on! I have on a few different eye shadow colors and lip blends by the time I turn and look at my pups. "What do you guys think?"

Cosmo whimpers and hides behind Rocket's hind legs.

I crack up. "Come on, it doesn't look that bad."

"What are you doing in my room?" Hurricane Marie is on the scene, and I'm standing in the eye of the storm. She seems calm, but I know better.

"You went through my stuff?" Marie walks over and grabs the tube of who-knows-what from my grip.

"I was just trying on a new look."

"Don't tell me this is for another one of your fund-raising ideas."

"It's for the Fall Formal."

Marie seems to soften even while she inspects her vanity for missing or broken cosmetics. "What's wrong with your old look?"

"I don't know if it'll work for the formal. I've never been to a dance before, so I don't know what to expect."

"Well, your usual look suits you more than how you look now," she says, eyeing my amateur makeover work.

I check out the mirror and don't recognize myself. I don't think I can pull off walking into the Fall Formal looking like this. The only change I should be working on right now is changing the shelter's fate.

"You're not wrong," I sigh, defeated.

Marie hands me some facial wipes, and I start by cleaning my eyelids.

"Does this formal focus mean you've finally given up trying to keep the shelter open?"

"No, of course not," I snap. "Can't I have more than one thing going at a time?"

"Not with how obsessed you've been about the rescues, no."

"I don't get you. Don't you love Cosmo and Rocket? They're rescues, too."

Marie looks in the mirror and puffs out a slow breath. When she speaks again, her voice starts off

soft, but grows more tense and loud. "I do love them, but I don't chase silly dreams to try to distract myself from reality. Bad things happen, and you can't always do something about it."

I hold back tears and shout, "At least I care about something enough to *do* something. All you care about is yourself and your precious image. Why don't you try doing something for someone *else* for a change? It may do you some good."

Both Marie and her reflection look at me, horrified. "What will do me some good is if you listen to me for once. Things don't always go the way you want them to. Disappointments happen, and it can hurt a lot

more if you don't prepare yourself for it. I've been let down before, so I know how that feels."

"At least I'm doing all I can. I may be too optimistic sometimes, but I know that helping the shelter stay open is important to me. There's a county budget meeting on Monday, and I plan to let my voice be heard so they vote yes for more funding."

"Go ahead. I think you *should* go down there. Whatever it takes to convince you that you're fighting a losing battle."

"You're the only loser here!"

"You know what? Get out of my room!" she thunders, pointing to the door.

"C'mon, guys, let's go."

Cosmo, Rocket, and I storm out as a group, and Marie slams her door behind us.

I storm out on sturdy legs, but when I shut the door to my own room, they feel like jelly. I'm not only rattled because of our fight. Marie and I have never knocked heads this hard before, and Mom and Dad would surely be disappointed if they had heard us. I'm also rattled because all the worst-case scenarios that I'd successfully avoided are starting to creep into my mind and haunt me.

If everything with the shelter goes horribly wrong, will I ever let myself fight this hard or care this deeply about another cause again?

♡🐺☆

As soon as I finish lunch, I grab my bike and ride over to the shelter. With Mom at the gallery and Dad on a long walk with Cosmo and Rocket, there's no way I want to stay home alone with Marie.

Ms. Keely gives me a warm hug when she sees me, and I know I've made the right choice.

After catching up with her for a quick minute, I go check up on Baby. The dog shuffles to the gate to lick my fingers grasping the chain-link fence, but I hardly crack a smile.

"I hope we don't let you down," I say to Baby. I don't know how I'll face these furry little friends if the town hall meeting doesn't play out like we all hope it will.

Chapter 14

There are way less people at the town hall meeting Monday evening than I thought there would be. My parents are with me. As for Marie . . . well, I'm not surprised she declined the invite. She didn't even have the courtesy to bow out to my face. She just gave me a muffled excuse through her bedroom door with the unwelcome sign on it.

Sam and Henry wanted to come, but they have rehearsal. Camila is at a family event, and Grace has to babysit her kid sister. So it's just me representing Mission: Rescue the Rescues.

I feel my mom's hand on my back as we look for a decent place to sit. We have plenty of options.

The posters I made over the weekend seem a little over the top in this place. The handful of people here are spread out over the mostly empty seats. There's a built-in wooden seating panel positioned a bit higher than the public seating area. County officials are taking their seats behind mics and settling in for what looks like a long, boring meeting ahead.

"*Psst* . . . Hope!"

How could I miss Ms. Keely's signature top bun in this thin crowd? I wave to her and lead my parents over to where she's sitting. They shake one another's

hands in greeting, and then I grab the seat between Ms. Keely and my mom.

On the other side of Ms. Keely is another shelter employee. I can tell because of his matching turquoise T-shirt.

I have my posters tucked in front of my legs, but Ms. Keely spots them. "Those images are beautiful!" she whispers. "Don't hide them."

I look at Mom, who nods in agreement. I take a deep breath, grab the posters, and stand up.

The posters are full-color images of Sam's pics

from the doggy photo shoot. They came out amazing! The first poster is of the tug-of-war over the rope toy. Above the image in big letters is the slogan:

We're Pulling for the Eastern Shore Animal Shelter!

The other is of the puddle-soaked pup, with the slogan:

They're in Deep. Please Help the Eastern Shore Animal Shelter!

The last is of Baby being a lazy lug:

No Sleep Until the Eastern Shore Animal Shelter Is Saved!

I feel like every set of eyes is staring at me as I

take them to the front, where the panel of officials can see them. I lean the posters against three empty seats in the front row. The couple of people nearby give me admiring looks. I guess it's not every day that a kid sits in on a county meeting.

"Nice job," someone in the audience says, smiling at me as I head back to my seat.

Something tells me it's going to take a lot more work to convince that panel of frown-faced officials sitting up there.

A half hour later, when the shelter funding is finally up for a vote, my hunch is proven correct.

"We've always supported the shelter in the past, but it's increasingly clear that any funding now would be like plugging a tiny hole in a sinking ship," says a man with a crooked tie. He seems like the top boss here, so of course, no other official speaks up with a different opinion.

Thank goodness they open up the floor for comments. The four people forming a short line behind the mic standing in the aisle next to my posters will present a different opinion.

First in line is Ms. Keely. She's standing tall with her chin up and hands resting on her hips. A shelter employee is behind her, followed by two community members who are here in support.

"Over the last year, we've built a strong network of volunteer professionals who have been generous with their time and skills," announces Ms. Keely. "At first, I wasn't sure that we could make it work. I volunteered at this shelter for a long time before I became the director, and I knew that it was in rough shape. It took a lot of knocking on doors and making phone calls. But what I found were many helping hands and big hearts. And you know what? That erased all of my doubts and strengthened my faith in this community. As a result of the help I received from the people of Brevard County, we now offer health

screenings, dog training, and grooming, in addition to adoption services. With your funding, we can continue building momentum and grow into a much stronger shelter *and* a much stronger community. Working on behalf of pets drew me closer to people, because pets show us our humanity; that's why today we are here, appealing to yours. Thank you."

"Thank you for your dedication," the official sitting at the far end says.

That's the biggest reaction of the meeting so far. It's like, do these officials even have emotions? I get up from my chair, and my parents give me a surprised look.

"Excuse me," I say, asking my parents to scooch

over their legs so I can squeeze by as the next people in line each say a few words. They do more than scooch over; they get up fast and give me full clearance. My parents each softly pat my back when I squeeze by.

I don't have any speech written up, and I'm not sure what I'll say. My mind races as I walk to the line. Thankfully, there's still one person ahead of me—a gray-haired man wearing a war veteran cap identical to my grandpa's. He finishes just as I arrive behind him.

"Tough crowd," cracks the veteran when he notices me behind him. I stand frozen. The fluttering in my stomach takes my mind back to Camila's larvae. But the empty space before the mic challenges me to step into it. After taking a deep breath, I do.

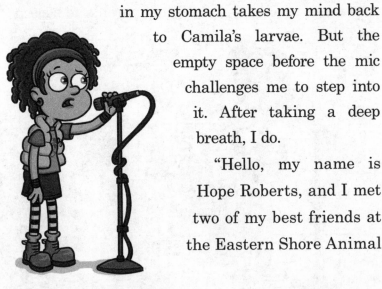

"Hello, my name is Hope Roberts, and I met two of my best friends at the Eastern Shore Animal

Shelter," I begin. "Yes, they're shelter dogs, but humans find shelter there, too. Everyone with a pet knows that warm bonding feeling. You feel loved, you feel less alone, you feel safe from all that worries you or scares you."

The sound of my amplified voice fills the space, all the way up to the high ceilings. Hearing it encourages me to go on.

"In fact, scratch that. My two rescue dogs aren't just my best friends. They're my *family*. Families come in all forms. And family members do *not* always look alike or act alike. Just ask my sister." I mumble the last part louder than expected. People in the audience softly chuckle, and a few members of the board almost smile.

"Families don't abandon each other in time of need," I continue. "My dogs once called the Eastern Shore Animal Shelter home, so I consider the rescues there my extended family. Standing up for Baby, Coco, Pixel"—I point to my posters propped against the chairs in the front row—"and all the others is like standing up for my family. And I don't know anyone who wouldn't try everything possible

to save their family. Family is about sticking together and supporting one another. And I stand here before you doing just that for mine. This money can help the shelter stay open. So I ask you today to please consider the impact closing the shelter will have, not only on these pets, but also on families in this community."

"Thank you, Miss Roberts. Your statement has been noted and will be taken into consideration."

I did it! I stood before a "tough crowd" and spoke up. My "statement has been noted" and everything. That sounds legit! I imagine my words written into the records of county history. It didn't even take Galaxy Girl–level courage. All I had to do was think of the shelter animals and speak from the heart.

The positive feels swirling inside me make my face tingle, and I smile to myself. When I walk back to my seat, there are proud, shining faces there to greet me.

"We've heard the public's statements and will take them into consideration as we put this to a vote now," says the boss man with the crooked tie.

I wonder if my words are enough to change the lawmakers' minds. The lump that forms in my throat would argue that it may not be.

The room goes quiet, and my mom reaches for my hand. I grip hers right back.

I prepare myself to watch each member on the committee rock forward, touch his or her lips to the mic with a yea or nay, and then lean back, self-satisfied.

"Yea," says the first member. My gleeful squeal ping-pongs against each wall, and everyone around me chuckles with relief.

My mom rubs my back and smiles a tight smile.

"Nay." The next member's vote interrupts our small celebration.

It's like the rest of the members

didn't let my words marinate. I think in the end,
that's why their votes sound so tasteless and bland.
None of the others vote yes.

Marie warned me this would happen.

The shelter isn't getting their funding.

Chapter 15

I beg my parents to skip the farewell gathering at the shelter and take me straight home instead. When I get to my room, I go right to my bed and lie awake there for a while. No checking my donation spreadsheet. No fund-raiser brainstorming. And no texting friends to check in on their Yappy Hour planning progress, either. Cosmo and Rocket sense something's up, so they lay off on their usual treat demands. Rocket even stays close, resting her head on my bed and nestling it next to mine.

When Dad comes in and leashes them for a walk, I pass on going with him.

"Hey, there's a cool new video out about the backstory of the black hole image," says Dad.

I know this is a test, but I don't take the bait. The truth is, I can't even summon the enthusiasm to talk about the black hole image, one of my all-time favorite topics.

Mom walks in, too, and sits at my bedside. She forces a cheery smile, but I can tell she feels sad for me. "How about I make you something to eat?"

"I'm not all that hungry," I say.

Marie is now standing in my doorway. "What's going on?"

I need someone on crowd control duty.

"I just need some space." My request comes out whinier than I'd hoped.

"Okay," Dad says gently, bending to kiss me on the forehead. "Take the time you need to let everything sink in. But you should know, you made us so proud, Hope."

Mom softly rubs my check with a finger. "It was a brave, selfless thing you did—standing up and using your voice to help this cause," she says. "You gave your all and you did your best."

"Thanks," I whisper to them. I appreciate them being comforting, but all I can focus on is visiting the shelter. I realize I want to hang around the only person who truly understands how I'm feeling— Ms. Keely. And it kinda isn't fair I'm not supporting her right now. She must be deeper in her feelings than I am.

I finally get up, and I'm thankful when my mom agrees to take me over to Ms. Keely's meet-up even though it's a school night.

When I get there, it's super clear to me Ms. Keely is taking things pretty hard, too. Her topknot is neatly slicked down, with nary a wayward strand floating anywhere. I nearly ask her for a glass of water to swallow down the shock.

"Mind if I take Hope for a stroll?" Ms. Keely asks Mom.

"She could probably use the fresh air and company," answers Mom with a gentle nod. Then she starts chatting to a few people she recognizes from the town hall meeting.

Ms. Keely walks me through the backyard exit door, away from the small crowd. We stop along the path to talk.

"I'm sorry I let you and the animals down," I say after a few moments of quiet.

"Hope, you should know you did the exact opposite of let us down," Ms. Keely says with a crack in her voice even as she has a comforting hand on my shoulder. "I think I've been pretty clear about how much energy and positivity you've brought to this place. I'm so grateful."

"A lot of good it did us." I roughly wipe away a tear. I'm somehow more angry than hurt.

She hands me a clean tissue from her back pocket. "Well, we still have that Yappy Hour you planned later this week. I'm coming, and so are a lot of friends of the shelter."

"Ugh, I don't even feel like going. Plus, I don't want to see . . . people. What's the point of even holding that anymore?" I look at Ms. Keely through my temporarily blurred vision.

"Are we doing this for Eastern Shore rescue dogs or rescue dogs in general? Just because it doesn't look good for *this* shelter doesn't mean we should stop fighting."

I sniff. "But what's the point in raising more money now?"

"You never know, we could get a big enough boost from the auction to keep the lights on for a few more weeks."

"And if we don't?"

"Simple." She throws up her hands. "We donate whatever we earn to another shelter. Every shelter needs steady community support to stay afloat. This could be a gift that saves another shelter from suffering the same fate."

"If Grace were here, she'd remind me to add that plan B donation info to the small print on our website."

"Sounds like your friend Grace's business sense is rubbing off on you."

"I guess that's true," I say, slowly nodding.

"Another Galaxite?"

The thought never occurred to me. "You know, I never asked."

"Now you know what to chat about the next time you see her." Ms. Keely winks at me, and I do something unexpected: I smile back. It's enough to remind me that everything is okay, or at least it will be soon enough.

Chapter 16

I can already tell all the prep work we did yesterday for the auction will pay off. Sam, Camila, Grace, Lacy, and Bella all help me set up Mom's gallery for

tonight's Yappy Hour, and I have to say, it looks great.

"Go, team!" I say, and hold out my hand for a high five.

Grace winks at the girls and then says, "Oh, come here!" They all pull me in for a group hug instead. When we've untangled ourselves and calmed down our giggles, I make the final rounds before we open the doors to guests.

Henry, Connor, and Shep set up the kennel cam livestream so it plays on the pull-down screen in the rear of the gallery. We all cheer when the pups come into view.

"Great job tonight," Henry congratulates me with a smile. "This setup is amazing."

"I couldn't have done it without all of you guys," I say, suddenly as bashful as Pixel the boxer. I walk away before I embarrass myself.

I continue walking around the gallery as more people arrive. There are table displays of auction items—a blender, an at-home spa basket, different electronics, Camila's doggy biscuits, Dad's NASA launch tickets, and more. Most of them were donated by local businesses or from friends and families who own businesses. The people in Lacy's mom's office building really came through.

But I happen to be wearing my favorite item here: Marie's fund-raiser fashion tees. She surprised the whole family with them before we left the house. It was like unwrapping a stylish birthday gift from your most glam friend. Mom, Dad, Sam—we all look extra cool wearing them.

That's what Marie had been working so hard on every morning at her sewing machine. And she crushed it. Her designs are beyond amazing. She found a way to make tiny paw prints look cute. There's a smattering of them over the cold shoulder design. It's better than something off the rack at your favorite store.

Despite all our bickering, my sister came through. I feel ashamed for thinking she wouldn't.

I watch as Bella and Marie have a sweet reunion. They hug each other and then jump into a nonstop conversation about fashion. I'm happy to see how excited they both are around each other.

"Thank you for making the shirts," I humbly say to Marie later when I see her setting out more fashion tees in the sale area at Mom's gallery. "They're dope."

"You're welcome," she says, not bothering to pause her activity. We haven't said much to each other since our big fight. Mostly because, since the county meeting, I've been avoiding her I-told-you-so's. It's too awkward to break through that now, but I will. And soon.

I continue fixing the subtle doggy-inspired decorations we sprinkled around the gallery. Camila's cupcakes look scrumptious. I'm so glad she agreed to bring some bakery treats for us humans. Yup. Everything is in place, and Mom's gallery looks beautiful.

Sure, it's hard to shake that this feels more like a consolation party. But if Ms. Keely can stay positive, if my parents, my sister, and my friends can show up here ready for a great night, then so can I.

As the event carries on, people stroll around, looking at the posters with my punny slogans and getting all the feels when watching the kennel livestream. My dad mingles and charms the crowd, and then Mom plays MC and grabs everyone's attention.

"We have an announcement that will come as a surprise to both Ms. Keely and Hope. Our top-selling item tonight is Marie Roberts's exclusive fashion tees, but Marie is also auctioning her styling services to one lucky student attending the JFK Middle School Fall Formal on Friday, and that item has seen the most active bidding tonight!"

Ms. Keely cheers with the crowd. I'm so touched, I cover my face in shock. Before I can see where I'm going, my legs carry me to Marie. When I see her, I run the rest of the way into her outstretched arms.

"Thank you so much," I say into her shoulder.

"I'm always here for you," she whispers. "Even if it's not in the way you expect."

"I know you were just protecting me from getting hurt, like you've been doing ever since I was a bullied kid on the playground," I sniff, pulling out of the hug but taking hold of one of her hands. "I understand that now."

"Hope," calls Dad's voice from behind me. "Someone would like to talk to you."

I turn to see him standing there with a cameraperson and a reporter carrying a microphone. My mom, Sam, Camila, and Grace are close behind them.

"What's this?"

"Hope, I'm a reporter from Channel Seven." The loud-spoken woman firmly shakes my hand. "We're covering the auction event tonight, and your parents here gave me permission to interview you—if you feel comfortable answering a few questions."

"That's fine with me." I look around for Ms. Keely and spot her across the gallery talking to a woman I don't recognize.

"Wonderful!" She signals to her cameraperson,

who hoists the large camera onto her shoulder. "Before I get started, may I say you have done an amazing job here. All the little touches are fabulous, too. I think I'm going to need to find out who made those cupcakes."

I catch Camila's eye and wink.

"Ready to roll," says the cameraperson.

"Okay, Hope. I'll just ask a few questions for playback during this evening's news."

Just as soon as I smooth back my hair and fix my shirt, the interview starts.

"Hope Roberts, I'm not sure you're aware, but your impassioned speech at the county budget meeting was captured on camera by local media and is

getting a lot of attention."

"You mean I went viral?" I ask, totally surprised. "No way!"

The reporter laughs. "Well, it certainly inspired many in our area, and I'm learning donations have doubled as a result," she said. My jaw wants to hang, but at the same time, I'm smiling.

This is such an emotional roller coaster of good then great news that my face must look like a rubbery mess.

"That's the best news I could've asked for," I say, my cheeks sore from smiling so hard. "Thank you to all who donated, adopted, and volunteered."

"And cut!" says the reporter. "You did great, Hope." Then she holds up her hand to summon Ms. Keely for her interview. "I wish you all the best."

I stand close to watch Ms. Keely's interview. And it's a good thing I do. Ms. Keely sees me and gives me an excited thumbs-up.

"Your efforts and Hope's speech have captured the attention of this area's most successful pet sanctuary, and I understand they've just offered to purchase the Eastern Shore Animal Shelter location!"

What?!

I'm stunned. Everyone erupts in cheers. My smile and jaw dropping tug-of-war is back, and I'm loving all the feels it's giving me.

"How does that sit with you?" the reporter asks Ms. Keely.

My mind is reeling as my parents sandwich me in a hug. We celebrate so loudly Ms. Keely has to shout into the microphone. "It's an amazing feeling to have such a happy ending after all the work everyone has done these past few months."

The minute the camera is off, I run to Ms. Keely, and she scoops me up in a hug.

"Can you believe this?" she squeals. "I was just talking to the owner of the rescue organization."

"I was wondering who that person was."

Ms. Keely's face beams as she nods. "I've been assured that all the cats and dogs will remain in their care until they're adopted."

"That's great!" I say, jumping in place.

"*So* great!"

"You did it!" I tell her.

"No, Hope. *We* did it."

☆

Chapter 17

When I get home on Friday afternoon, it feels like I have the weight of the last few weeks on my shoulders. I drop my backpack on my bed after school, and it falls on a dress.

Wait. A dress?

I slide it out from under my bag and am floored by what I see. It's a sleeveless, scoop neck dress with a full skirt that's screen printed with Cosmo's and Rocket's pics in black and white.

"Marie," I whisper. And

then I squeal at the top of my lungs, "Marie!"

Mom, Dad, and Marie run in, cameras in hand, and go paparazzi.

"How did you—?"

Mom and Dad put their arms around each other and give off that prideful vibe again.

Marie claps and cracks up. "I had to sneak around behind your back and hide it in my closet. That day I caught you in my room, you almost blew the surprise."

"Yeah, and I was a class act that day." I cringe at the insult-hurling memory. "I'm so sorry, Marie, for everything."

"I'm sorry, too."

Mom starts singing the wacky song she made up when we were small. "The sisterhood . . . Yeah, life is good . . ."

"Um, Marie's gotta go style her auction winner soon, so I better change into this quick." I shoo Dad, Mom, and the singing out the door.

"Yeah, and I better stay to help her, so bye-bye, fam jam," she says in a small voice.

When they're both out, we squeal and laugh some more.

Sometimes Marie and I are on the same team, and it's a good feeling.

♡🐺☆

It's finally the Fall Formal, and all my friends are here. There's a cool photo booth Grace and Bella ordered, and we're all lined up to take pics in it.

☆ 186 ☆

"Everyone will get a chance if you line up," Bella calls out to the small crowd. She's dressed as cool as you can imagine in a floral print dress. Grace is beside her in a pink jumpsuit that matches her glasses.

Sam and I inch up in line, checking out each other's dresses, just like we did our first-day-of-school outfits. Her flowy purple dress looks retro cool. I'm pretty sure it's vintage.

"You look ah-mazing!" she screeches.

"You look beautiful!" I tell her at the same time. We both laugh.

"You have your sister, and I have the theater costume closet!" She grins. "Wait until you see how we dress for the musical."

"I can't wait to see it," I say. Her opening night is in a few short weeks. I already know Sam will be a showstopper, so JFK Middle better get ready.

Henry and Archie join the crowd, and both walk over when they spot us.

"Hi, Hope," says Henry, looking . . . um, different— in a good way. He's wearing a button up instead of a basketball jersey.

"Hi." I smile at him.

"Sam, want to take a picture together?" Archie, in a bow tie, asks my best friend.

"Sure, yes, uh-huh," Sam answers all at once.

Henry and I watch them pose side by side together. I glance at Henry's profile. When I look away, he glances my way. And this time when Henry's shoulder bumps mine, it's not by accident. I break out in a bashful smile. Before I know it, Henry is snapping a selfie of us.

"Get in here!" Sam waves Henry and me over for a group pic. Henry puts away his phone and follows me into the booth. Sam, Archie, Henry, and I all huddle and say cheese.

"Hey, I'm next after them," I hear Connor say to the photographer. He walks over after our group is done and waits for the photographer to be ready.

Feeling awkward standing there with Henry and Connor, I make small talk. "Guess we won't be needing that kennel cam anymore now that the dogs are in good hands."

"Duh," Connor says. "I can see that you're in advanced classes."

I sigh. "I walked right into that one," I mumble under my breath.

"I can help you uninstall it," says Henry, and my face gets hot. "Uh, you know, so I can see the dogs again."

"R-right. I miss them, too," I say.

"Pshaw, I don't have to worry about that problem," Connor says in his best boastful voice. "Because I just adopted Pixel earlier today. I get to see her all the time!"

"Next!" the photographer calls out. Connor steps up to be photographed.

Everyone congratulates Connor. I get the feels in spite of this being *Connor's* big moment. Hey, I'd have to be a robot not to.

Camila and Grace walk up beside me, and Camila gives my arm a squeeze. "You helped make his doggy adoption happen," she says.

That reminds me of something Ms. Keely told me.

"Just a few drops is all it takes to keep the flow of progress going," I tell her, thinking of the impact of our Rescue the Rescues mission and my town hall speech. *Why stop now when we can help make a difference at JFK Middle, too?*

"Is that in our science book?" Camila asks.

"No, but I think I'll put it in my playbook when I run for sixth-grade president," I say out loud for the first time.

"I hear that," says Grace. "Need a campaign manager?"

I reach out my hand, 100 percent expecting Grace to shake it. Thankfully, she doesn't leave me hanging. I give her a grin, and then we all head to the booth for a group pic.

A photo booth today, the voting booth tomorrow. And I can't wait!

HOPE'S TIPS

Hot dog! Finding homes for my furry friends wasn't easy, but in the end, it was all worth it. Caring for your community rocks. Not only are you helping the people (or animals) you see every day, but you can have fun doing it, too! Whether the cause is something small (like helping a person in need) or big (like raising money for an animal shelter), it's so important to get involved. After all, that's the first step to changing the world.

Here are some tips on how you can help out your favorite causes, too!

Spread the word: Raise awareness by sharing your goals with family and friends. They may be able to brainstorm ideas with you or even lend a hand. But don't stop there! Creating flyers, posters, and social media posts about your cause can take things up a notch. Remember, giving back is a group effort.

Raise money: Fundraising is an important part of giving back, but it doesn't happen on its own. Try setting up a donation collection in your community, holding a charity auction, or partnering with a larger charitable organization to raise money for the cause.

Use your voice: Being an advocate for a cause takes a lot of speaking up at gatherings and events. Talk to the right people—whether it's the head of an organization, the city council, or even your congresspeople. But don't worry if you're not a great public speaker. You can write letters and emails, too.

Volunteer: Helpers are valuable to a community, so sign-up to volunteer! Sometimes there are age restrictions, but you can always team up with a parent or older sibling to pitch in. From participating in neighborhood clean-ups and collecting cans for a local food pantry, to planning and helping out at an event, every role is important. Volunteers make a difference, one small act at a time.

Do what you do best: Lean on your own special interests and strengths to help further the cause. Are you a writer? Send letters to help spread the word. A baker? Whip up some treats for a bake sale fundraiser. Whatever you do, you've got this!

About the Author

Dirk Franke

ALYSSA MILANO began acting when she was only 10 years old. She has continued to work in both TV and movies since then, including hit shows like *Who's the Boss?* and *Charmed.* Alyssa is also a lifelong activist who is passionate about fighting for human rights around the world. She has been a National Ambassador for UNICEF since 2003, and she enjoys speaking to students in schools around the country about the importance of voting. She was named one of *Time* magazine's Persons of the Year in 2017 for her activism. Alyssa lives in Los Angeles with her husband and two kids. This is her first children's book series.

About the Author

DEBBIE RIGAUD is the coauthor of Alyssa Milano's Hope series and the author of *Truly Madly Royally*. She grew up in East Orange, New Jersey, and started her career writing for entertainment and teen magazines. She now lives with her husband and children in Columbus, Ohio. Find out more at debbierigaud.com.

About the Illustrator

ERIC S. KEYES is currently an animator and character designer on *The Simpsons*, having joined the show in its first season. He has worked on many other shows throughout the years, including *King of the Hill*, *The Critic*, and *Futurama*. He was also a designer and art director on Disney's *Recess*. Hope is his first time illustrating a children's series. Eric lives in Los Angeles with his wife and son.